SYD

SISTERS BY DESIGN BOOK 5

SHARON SROCK

A BLONDE AND A PRAYER BOOKS

For my granddaughter Hailey. You came into this world a tiny thing. Three and a half pounds of love. You have grown into a beautiful woman with a big smile and a huge heart.
"...Those who seek the Lord lack no good thing."
Psalms 34:10

ACKNOWLEDGMENTS

As always, first thanks goes to my Heavenly Father for the story and for the words. I hope I got it right. If one person finds encouragement in the pages of Syd's story, to You be all glory!

A special thanks to Ronda Wells, MD. When I sent out the SOS for help with Logan's illness, she responded with some great input. When the story took a twist and I didn't need him to be as ill as I first expected, she helped me figure that out as well. If I deviated from her directions, let that be on me. When it comes to photography, I'm clueless. Mo Shultz was a fount of information.

I can never say thank you enough to the wonderful team of professionals God has placed on my team and the group of prayer partners He has surrounded me with. You make all the difference, and you are appreciated beyond words.

If a writer has a family that supports, even when they don't understand, they are blessed. I am blessed beyond measure. For all the times I bored you with a story, took "our" time for "story" time, or simply zoned out of a real conversation because the fictional one happening in my head was too loud...thanks for loving me anyway.

ALSO BY SHARON SROCK

THE VALLEY VIEW SERIES:
CALLIE
TERRI
PAM
SAMANTHA
KATE KARLA
HANNA'S ANGEL
A MAKEOVER MADE IN HEAVEN

THE MERCIE COLLECTION:
FOR MERCIE'S SAKE
BEGGING FOR MERCIE
ALL ABOUT MERCIE

SISTERS BY DESIGN:
MAC
RANDY
CHARLEY
JESSE
SYD

CHAPTER 1

"That's ridiculous. How could you not know your husband was taking advantage of your daughter?"

Sydney Patterson cringed as the hot sting of shame crept up the back of her neck. She inched the cart closer to the register and sent a hesitant glance over her shoulder. Some of the weight lifted when she saw that the two women behind her were looking at one of the gossip rags displayed by the checkout lane, not at her.

She blew out a deep breath.

Would she ever be completely free? The self-condemnation for things she hadn't thought possible, the bite of betrayal, the slow slide into a pit of despair without a handhold, the memory of people she loved looking at her as if she were an intentional idiot instead of an unwitting victim.

"Did you find everything?"

The chipper question interrupted the memories, and Syd found herself grateful. She smiled at the girl scanning her groceries. "I did, thanks."

The girl pulled items from the belt and kept up a running monologue as she dragged them across the scanner. "These cookies are great, aren't they? Havarti slices? I've never tried that type of cheese on a sandwich. Is it good? I need to try this new creamer. We're sure selling a lot of it."

It wasn't necessary for Syd to respond. A friendly nod seemed good enough to keep the girl going.

"Oh, look at these nice steaks." The girl winked. "Someone's having a party."

That drew a genuine smile. Syd was fixing dinner for Mason tonight. Sort of a welcome to Garfield celebration. Syd had met Mason at Jesse's and Mac's big wedding six months ago. That wasn't a night she'd forget soon. A double wedding for two of her friends, a madman with a gun, and Mason.

Mason Saxton. His name made something tingle inside her, something that Syd would have sworn had died a horrible and tragic death years ago. The man was wickedly good looking with his lean face, cleft chin, salt-and-pepper hair, eyes a shade of blue that rivaled the Pacific Ocean off the coast of Oahu, and just a touch of scruff. He was also the father of Jesse's groom, Garrett. He'd been in town for the wedding and surrounded by people he didn't know. As part of Syd's wedding weekend duties, she'd been assigned the task of keeping Mason occupied.

She rolled her eyes. That was not a chore assigned by chance. Her friends had obviously had romance on the brain.

But Mason-duty hadn't been all bad. Not only was he easy to look at, his personality and charm matched his good looks. When he'd asked for permission to call her once he got home to San Antonio, her initial hesitation gave way to *why not*. After all, San Antonio, Texas, was a long way from Garfield, Oklahoma. She'd felt safe with that. And then, over the months of calls and emails, they'd grown comfortable with each other. They had a lot in common—both widowed, both dealing with empty nests, both fairly new believers.

When he'd told her he was moving to Garfield, the news had forced Syd to take a hard look at this new friendship. She'd kept her distance from men for eight years. But Sara and Logan were in their own home now, and Ginny, well, her younger daughter's situation wasn't likely to change any time soon. Syd could afford a friendship with a man, as long as she didn't let it go any deeper than that.

"Is that everything you need today?"

Once again the checker's friendly voice pulled Syd out of her musings. "I think so."

The girl smiled, gave her a total, and waited for Syd to swipe her debit card. She held out a receipt. "You have a good evening."

In her peripheral vision Syd watched the woman in line behind her put the gossip rag back in the rack and motion to it before pushing her cart forward. "Ludicrous, I tell you. Absolutely ludicrous. There's no way that sort of behavior could happen right under your nose and you not see it." Her friend put a hand over her heart and nodded in agreement.

Syd turned her back and walked away. *I pray you never find out differently.*

* * *

MASON SCOOTED the couch into the corner of his newly rented home in Garfield late on Friday afternoon and studied it. "What do you think?"

The golden retriever at his side sank down and laid his head on his paws. Doleful chocolate brown eyes shifted from him to the sofa and back again.

"That bad, huh?" He grabbed one end, placed it on a diagonal angle, and stepped back.

The dog gave a soft chuff.

"Yeah, that's just in the way."

Mason looked around at the mess of furniture and boxes and concluded that everything from his oversized four bedroom home in San Antonio wasn't going to fit into the modest three-bedroom ranch he now called home. A storage facility was his only hope. As luck would have it, those businesses were as plentiful in this part of the country as spots on a blue tick hound. He glanced at the furniture and boxes he needed to store. The majority of it had belonged to Elaine. The thought didn't sting as much as it had in the past. Storing her stuff wasn't the same as getting rid of it.

When the doorbell rang, the dog jumped to his feet. His nails clicked as he skittered across the tile of the entry. He scratched at the threshold, barking his intruder alert.

"Brody, no!"

The dog ignored the command. Typical.

Mason hurried to the door, tossing the space issue aside for now. It wasn't as if he had to have the boxes unpacked, the books shelved, and the pictures hung before bedtime. That had been Elaine's compulsion, not his. But, he glanced at the framed prints leaning against the wall. Maybe he would make time for his pictures before the day was over. Since he'd discovered a passion for photography, the shots he'd taken—of trees, mountains, valleys, sunrises, and sunsets—always brought him a sense of peace. Even before he'd fully recognized those beautiful things as God's creation, he'd found peace in nature. He needed that in this new place.

"Brody, sit."

The dog sat and the barking decreased to a whine.

Mason opened the door to find his son on the stoop. The aroma coming from the brown bag in his hand made Mason forget everything except the fact that he hadn't eaten since breakfast.

"How's it going, Pops?" Garrett asked.

"Pitifully until now." Mason reached for the bag. "I'm so hungry I could eat a bowl of Brody's kibble."

Garrett handed over the Sonic bag along with the large milkshake he held in the other hand. "You do know there's a Sonic just two miles away. The grocery store is even closer. If you're starving, you've no one to blame but yourself." He stooped to take the dog's ears in his hands and rocked Brody's head from side to side. "On the job, I see."

"Loud and proud and absolutely no help with these boxes." Mason jerked his head in the direction of the kitchen and wound his way through the maze of boxes. "We've been trying to figure out where everything should go."

"Your conclusions?"

"It's hopeless." Mason sat at the cluttered table, pulled out the burger and fries, and arranged them on the wrapper while Brody curled into a ball beneath his chair. The dog was no dummy. He knew there was a snack in his future if he stayed close. Mason nodded to a second chair. "You have time to sit?"

Garrett cleared a box from the chair and lowered his tall frame into it. "For a few. Jesse gets off work in an hour, and I promised to pick her up."

"Something wrong with her car?"

"Her alternator quit on her yesterday. I'm her chauffer till the shop calls."

Mason answered with a grunt, chased the burger with a healthy slurp of his shake, and swallowed. "And you love it." He dropped a fry on the floor. Brody snapped it up as if he were going for a land speed record.

"I love that she understands I'm not a car guy. It's a great thing to find a woman who accepts your limitations."

Mason swiped a couple of fries through the catsup. "She's a keeper." He pushed away from the table. "Speaking of keepers. I'll be right back." He left the kitchen and returned with a heavy box. He set it on the floor next to Garrett's feet. "This is for you guys."

Garrett bent over the box, parted the flaps, and lifted out a layer of bubble wrap. A quiet gasp escaped him. "Mom's china?"

"She'd want you two to have it."

"But—"

"It's been five years, and I'm still carting around your mother's things." He swallowed. "Time to take some baby steps toward my future." His thoughts went to a certain blonde who was fixing dinner for him this evening. Maybe it was time for more than just baby steps.

"I don't disagree, Dad." Garrett unwrapped a cup and fingered the delicate blue design etched into the white edge. "Jesse and I will treasure this." The sadness turned to a grin. "This mess would drive Mom loco."

Mason glanced at the cluttered space. "I was just thinking the same thing. We only moved three times in our thirty-one years of marriage, but we never went to bed on the first night in a new place with boxes stacked in the corner. Your mother was a little maniac when it came to organization. And she didn't care who she had bully to get it done."

Both men were quiet for a moment as memories drifted through Mason's mind.

"I miss her," Garrett whispered. "I'd stay here all night and help you unpack if it meant seeing her smile one more time."

Mason's throat clogged with emotion. He clapped his son on the back. "I'm gonna stack all of your mother's stuff out in the garage for now. There are a few more things I think she'd like you and your bride to have. I'll make a pile for you and Jesse to go through when you get the chance." He surveyed what he could see of the boxes, mentally judging the contents. "If I do that, I might actually be able to turn around in here by next week without tripping over a piece of furniture."

Garrett stood, stooped to retrieve the box of china, and headed to the front door. "I need to head that way or face Jesse's wrath at being left on the curb. I'm supposed to ask you if you want to come for dinner."

"You tell that bride of yours I said thanks, but I have plans."

Garrett met his dad's gaze. "Those plans wouldn't involve a pretty blonde named Syd, would they?"

"And if they did?"

His son studied him for a few seconds. "I had the best mom in the world, and no one could replace her. But I'm learning how much of a blessing it is to have someone special in your life. If she makes you happy, you have my complete blessing."

* * *

SYD MOVED from dessert preparation to salad to checking the steaks on the grill. She came back in the house, fanning a dishtowel at a couple of flies determined to follow her in.

"Get out of here."

The early September temperature hovered around eighty degrees, her main reason for choosing the grill over heating up the house. The microwaved potatoes, freshly chopped salad, and no-bake fruit trifle rounded out her menu and kept the temperature in the house pleasant for a nice long visit.

I'm entertaining a man in my house.

A year ago, the thought of it, much less the reality, would have been incomprehensible. But now that Sara had finished college, landed a decent job, and moved her and Logan into their own place, Syd had some freedom she hadn't known she'd missed. Hadn't even dreamed of needing until Mac's and Jesse's double wedding six months ago.

When Mason asked for her phone number, she'd assumed he was just being polite. The first call four nights later surprised her, and she'd found herself both flattered and flustered by the attention. They'd talked for an hour, rehashing the events of the wedding. Him, pleased and proud of his son, she, excited for her friends and the lives they'd just begun. Soon the calls became a nightly ritual, something she looked forward to at the end of a long day at the bank like she would a long soak in a hot tub with a riveting book.

He talked about his job and life in San Antonio. She learned about his marriage to Elaine and the pain of her loss five years earlier. In the spirit of sharing, she'd talked about her years with Anthony. Those golden years of being a stay-at-home mom, pampered and adored by a good man.

She'd picked through the events of her more recent history like a war refugee walking through an abandoned minefield, convincing herself that an unspoken truth wasn't a lie, just a matter of privacy. She told Mason all about the business courses she'd taken in preparation for her first job, about the shock of Sara's pregnancy at the age of fifteen, the world-changing love of becoming a grandmother, and the absolute joy Logan brought into her life. There was more to the story...of course there was. But none of her friends knew those parts. Mason didn't need to know either.

The sound of a car in the driveway brought her gaze to the kitchen window. Mason climbed out of his black Buick, stooped to reach back inside, and emerged with a single red rose in a vase. The sight of that solitary flower did something funny to Syd's insides. No one had brought her flowers since Anthony's death.

Syd dried her hands on a kitchen towel, reached up to check her hair, and took the time to smooth the orange-and-yellow geometric print tunic she'd paired with brown jeans and sandals. She hadn't seen Mason since the wedding, and maybe she was being foolish, but at some point over the last six months, his opinion of her had become important.

She hurried to the front door and had it open by the time Mason stepped onto the cement porch.

"You're right on time."

Mason stopped and studied her, the corners of his blue eyes crinkling when he smiled. "No one in their right mind is late for a steak dinner prepared by a beautiful woman." He took two more steps and offered the rose. "For you."

Syd reached for the flower, amazed to see her hand trembling. "It's lovely, thank you."

"Not as lovely as you."

Mason's words sent heat up the back of Syd's neck. She bowed her head and gave herself two deep breaths, inhaling the blossom's fragrance and hoping that the blush dissipated quickly.

Good grief. He'll think I'm a ninny straight out of high school.

The timer on her cell phone sounded. Syd pulled it from her pocket and silenced the noise. "Steaks should be done. Come on in while I get them off the grill."

Mason followed her to the kitchen. "What can I do to help?"

Syd set the vase on the counter and snagged a platter and a fork on her way out the back door. She nodded toward the two glasses sitting on the cabinet next to the fridge. "You can put ice in those glasses and pour the tea. I'll be right back."

When she came back in, she found that Mason had poured the tea and placed the rose in the center of the table.

"Look at you," Syd said, pleased with his thoughtfulness.

He took the platter from her, placed it on the table, and pulled out a chair. "Allow me."

Syd took her seat and grinned as he settled across from her. "You need to be careful."

"About...?"

"Spoiling me so thoroughly on your first day in town. I might decide I like it."

His grin answered hers. "Good." He motioned to the meal. "This looks amazing. Would you like me to say a blessing?"

"Please." Syd took the hand he offered and fought to ignore the little jolt of attraction the contact generated. There were a lot of things she could get used to where Mason Saxton was concerned.

When he finished, she cut a piece of her steak and looked up before putting it in her mouth. "How's the unpacking going?"

Mason chuckled. "It's miserable. This is the first time I've tried to set up housekeeping without Elaine. I'm learning that I'm not very good at it. I moved the couch four times today, and I still don't like it."

Syd chewed and wondered if offering to help him would be too much, too soon.

"I'm about to concede defeat. You wouldn't care to give a helpless man a few pointers, would you?"

Well, that was a handy and timely request. Syd considered her weekend schedule. She had plans with Logan tomorrow. She'd seen her grandson every day for the first seven years of his life. She missed that now that he and Sara were living on their own. Sunday had its own challenges, but Monday…she could make that work. She must have hesitated too long.

"I'm sorry," Mason said. "I'm asking too much of our friendship."

"Don't be silly. I was just thinking about my schedule. Would Monday evening work for you?"

"Monday is perfect. I have some things to drop off at the Salvation Army after I meet with my new boss. I should be home by six-thirty."

"Your boss? I thought you had next week free to settle in."

"He's going out of town for a couple of weeks. He wanted a chance to show me around before he leaves. Do you like Chinese? I'll get take out."

"You don't have to feed me."

"I insist."

"Then yes, I like Chinese."

The rest of their dinner progressed in comfortable conversation. They'd grown accustomed to regular chats, but the face to face aspect added a new dimension of pleasure for Syd.

Mason scooped up the last bite of his dessert and leaned back in his chair. "Talk about spoiling. I haven't had a meal like that in a very long time. Will you let me help you with the dishes?"

"Only if you insist," Syd answered with a laugh. "I love to cook, but I hate the cleanup."

Together they carried dishes into the kitchen. He rinsed them, and she loaded the dishwasher. *Is there anything* not *to like about this man?* As Syd reached for the dish towel to give the countertop a final swipe, her phone rang. A look at the screen sent her eyebrows arching under her bangs.

Rita Marlin? The woman hadn't initiated a call to her in years. The last time had been when Ginny fell off a horse and broke her collar bone.

Ginny. The dinner she'd just enjoyed gave her a rebellious nudge. Syd swallowed. "Excuse me, I have to take this," she told Mason before rushing to her bedroom. With a closed door at her back, she swiped the call open with trembling hands. "Rita, is something wrong with Ginny?"

"No, Ginny's fine. I...you..."

Syd frowned while she waited for Anthony's mother to continue. The woman sounded old...confused...not at all the vibrant, take-charge woman who'd finished ripping Syd's family apart eight years ago.

A throat cleared on the other end of the line. "Ginny is fine. But Harold is not."

"What's wrong," Syd asked.

"Harold had a heart attack last night."

Anthony's father. He'd always been the strong but silent type. He'd backed his wife's bid for custody of Ginny, but he'd never spewed the venom in Syd's direction that Rita had. "I'm sorry. Is there anything I can do?"

"He'll be fine," Rita ignored the offer of help. Syd had known she would. Rita had long considered Syd to be beneath her. "He'll require a triple bypass and a lengthy recuperation. His doctor recommended a complete change of lifestyle. We've decided to move our retirement plans up. To do that..."

The woman paused, and Syd could picture her chewing her lip and pacing in front of the old fashioned landline house phone.

"Well…we can't keep up with an active teenager. Your daughter needs to come home."

Syd sucked in air, flooded with joy at the thought of having her youngest child home. Joy turned to dread at the thought of having her youngest daughter home. No one in her new life knew about Ginny.

Syd closed her eyes as shame flooded over her. *What kind of a mother are you?* A broken one, she admitted to herself as she took down flight information for the next day. She thanked her former mother-in-law, disconnected the call, and looked at the phone with tears in her eyes. Her baby was coming home.

A muffled cough filtered in from another part of the house.

Mason. Syd clutched the phone to her chest. What was she going to do about Mason? This evening had been a dream come true, one she'd anticipated repeating. That would be impossible now. One phone call had turned her new found joy to dust. She needed him out of the house, she needed to call Sara. She needed to decide what came next.

Tell him the truth.

Syd snorted at the random thought. Telling him, or anyone else, the unabridged truth about her past was out of the question. She squared her shoulders. Her daughter was coming home, and her barely begun friendship with Mason Saxton was ending tonight. She took a deep breath, schooled her face, and reached for the doorknob as the carefully constructed foundation of her life in Garfield cracked beneath her.

CHAPTER 2

"*A*re you excited?"

Syd didn't answer Sara's question for a few seconds. Navigating the traffic into Will Rogers World Airport was always tedious. The construction around the huge complex only added an additional layer of lip chewing. She picked her lane from the overhead signs and followed the one leading to hourly parking. Once committed, she glanced at her oldest daughter.

"Honestly? More nervous than excited. Eight years is a long time. I know we've flown out to Utah for regular visits, but Ginny has to feel like her life is being upended a second time. I never wanted that. As much as I longed to have her back, that's one of the reasons I never petitioned for custody after I lost her. I didn't want her to have to readjust all over again."

Syd stopped to wait for a departing car to vacate the perfect parking spot and looked at her watch. "And we're an hour early." She glanced in the rearview mirror. Her ex-husband's eyes met hers, and her heart lurched.

Breathe.

She obeyed the internal command and pulled a steadying

breath into her lungs. The momentary lapse had to be due to Ginny's return and the memories it dredged up. She loved her grandson with her whole heart. It wasn't Logan's fault that he sometimes looked or acted like her deceitful second husband. Half of the child's DNA came from him.

When she looked again, Logan's gap-toothed, freckle-faced smile brightened her mood. There were many things she would change about the past, but this child wasn't one of them. This child was the perfect example of the beauty for ashes God's word promised. "We've got some time. You want to go in, get a soda, and see if we can find a spot to watch the planes?"

"Yes!"

Syd heard the snap of his seatbelt unbuckling. Apparently, Sara did too.

"Logan Edward Marlin, put that seatbelt back on until your grandmother has parked this car."

"Yes, ma'am."

When the child had complied, Syd lowered her voice and cut a glance at her daughter. "A three-name offense?"

"Everything is a three name offense these days. I guess I should be happy to see some enthusiasm out of him for a change."

"Oh?"

"It's that stupid video game I bought him for his birthday. I swear that's all he's interested in. He barely eats, says he isn't hungry. If I suggest going outside, he's too tired, but every time I look for him, he's sprawled on the bed glued to the screen."

They exited the car, took a short ride on the moving walkway, rode the escalator up, and came into the main part of the building. Logan darted here and there, excited about exploring a new place. Syd put an arm around her daughter's shoulders. "He seems fine today. It's only been a month since his birthday. The new will wear off the games eventually."

"I hope so," Sara answered before jogging a few steps ahead to keep her inquisitive son in sight.

Syd found the check-in counter for the airline Ginny was traveling on and because Ginny was a minor and flying by herself for the first time secured clearance to meet her at the gate. She and Sara settled into vinyl seats with their drinks while Logan sat on the floor in front of the large window and watched the planes come and go.

Sara watched her son while Syd chewed her lip and picked at a hangnail. She jumped when Sara put a hand over hers.

"It's going to be OK," Sara told her. "And even if Ginny isn't thrilled about the circumstances, she's old enough to understand this isn't your fault."

Syd pursed her lips and stared at a distant point outside the window. "I know you're right, but she just started her senior year. I can't forget the excitement in her voice when she called to tell me about the college plans she and her friends were making."

"And I remember the disappointment in your eyes when you told me that she hadn't left any time in her schedule for us to visit between graduation and college."

"It's not her fault that we aren't as close as I'd like."

"I know Grandma and Grandpa thought they were doing the right thing for Ginny at the time..." Sara scoffed, a short puff of air to reveal her displeasure. "But you are our mother. You deserve better than second place in her life."

Syd closed her eyes. *What do I deserve?* She tried to balance one daughter's loyalty with the other's lack. The scales would never be even, not with the guilt she could never put behind her.

Why do you wallow in things I've forgotten?

Syd's eyes filled behind her closed eyelids. That gentle touch to her spirit and the peaceful voice in her heart always made her feel loved...even when she couldn't love herself.

I know, Father. I wish my memory could be as forgiving as Yours. It was just so ugly.

Trust me, daughter. I make all things beautiful in its time.

"Lookie."

Logan's excited voice yanked Syd back to the present.

"Is that Auntie Ginny?"

Syd watched the twin jet airliner slide up to the jet way. "I bet it is. Come stand by us so she can see us all at once."

Logan scrambled to his feet and hurried to Syd's side. "Just wait till she sees how big I got! Bet she won't even know it's me."

She ruffled his straight blond hair and tried to pump up excitement over trepidation. Her baby was coming home. These weren't the circumstances Syd would have chosen, and there would be a lot of...selective explaining...but her baby was coming home. In that moment, Syd discovered that it was possible to be thrilled and scared spitless at the same time. She watched the doorway, and longing tugged at her when Ginny entered the terminal. Short and petite like Sara, the blond hair she shared with her sister and her mother was cut into a spikish do with the ends tipped in hot pink. Syd blinked and wondered what Ginny'd had to do to talk her conservative grandmother into that?

Logan broke into a run, his sneakers squealing on the tile floor as he skidded to a stop in front of his aunt. "Boo!"

Ginny jerked to a stop and put a hand over her heart. "Oh, you scared me." She put her hands on her hips and leaned down. "Who are you?"

The boy giggled. "Logan."

"No, the only Logan I know is a short little pipsqueak. You're almost a man. Maybe I'm dreaming." She gave the boy's shoulder a quick, playful pinch.

"Hey," Logan rubbed the spot. "What'd you do that for?"

"Just making sure you were real." She gathered the little boy close. When she stood, she held his hand as they approached. Ginny gave Sara a smile. "Hey, sis."

Sara held her arms out, and Ginny stepped into them. "Welcome home. How's Grandpa?"

Ginny stepped out of the hug. "Better, I guess. Between them being at the hospital, then the rush to get me on a plane, I haven't talked very much to either of them since all this started."

Syd touched Ginny's arm. "I know you're worried, baby, but I'm sure he'll be OK."

Ginny looked at her mother, and Syd almost cringed at the ice in her youngest daughter's stare.

"Yeah, well." Ginny turned her back and held out a hand to her nephew. "Come on, sport, let's go find my luggage."

Bereft, Syd watched her go. Ginny'd had no hug or smile of greeting for her mother. *Umm...God. About that timing thing...*

* * *

MASON STIRRED sweetener into his coffee on Saturday morning and replayed the final few minutes of his evening with Syd.

What had he done?

Well, OK, he wasn't a total moron. He understood that the phone call Syd had received brought about the sudden change in her behavior, but still...

He carried his cup to the living room and set it on the table next to his recliner. The hulking black chair was about twenty years old. Designed for the "big and tall" man, the scarred leather chair knew every crease and dent in his middle-aged backside. Elaine had begged him to get rid of it for years, but one didn't discard an old friend simply because there was a new and improved model.

Mason sat, twisted a bit to the left to avoid the poke of a worn out spring, and surveyed his work. He wasn't anywhere near done, but he'd made progress. Between the framed prints of his photos and this beat up old chair, his new house was beginning to feel like a home. He picked up his cup and blew steam from the top before risking a deep swallow of the sweet, creamy concoction.

I should be working. True enough, but when a man had questions on his mind, he deserved one quiet cup of coffee to start his day.

Brody had other ideas. He dashed into the living room, skidded to a stop, and dropped a well-worn, drool soaked ball into Mason's lap. The dog sat and stared at his master. Mason picked the ball up with two fingers and lobbed it across the room. "It's too early. We'll have a game of ball later." Brody retrieved the ball and returned it to Mason's lap. This time the dog crouched, front legs down, hind end up, tail wagging in anticipation. *Woof!*

Mason grunted. "You're pushy, you know that?"

Brody straightened and laid his head on Mason's knee. The soft whine he emitted almost sounded scolding.

Maybe the dog had a point. A little fresh air could only enhance his brooding. Coffee in one hand, soggy ball in the other Mason followed Brody to the back door. Once on the porch he balanced his cup on the rail and tossed the ball into the far corner of the giant, fenced backyard. It landed in some tall decorative plants and Mason had a few moments to enjoy his caffeine while Brody sniffed out the ball.

Mason had come a long way for a fresh start, following a yearning to find a place where everyone and everything didn't remind him of Elaine. Not that he wanted to forget the woman he'd loved or the thirty-one years they'd had together—he'd rather cut off his right hand. But the constant reminder of loss, living in a place where he expected to see her in every corner of every room, shopping in the same stores, eating at the same restaurants. It was tedious, a life Mason had chewed all the flavor out of a long time ago. He needed a change. Change, when it presented itself, came in a twofold package. A relocation opportunity close to his only son—and Sydney Patterson.

Six months later his attraction to Syd remained a pleasant surprise. He had friends back in San Antonio who'd begun a long-term campaign to set him up with a *nice woman*. Nice women abounded, but none had captured his attention like Syd.

Mason Leland Saxton was many things, but no one could accuse him of being a foolish old man. He wasn't some green kid with a crush, rushing to uproot his life at the first sniff of companionship, but the promise of their friendship had been a nice side benefit of the move. A side benefit that, Mason tossed the ball for the dog, he wasn't going to let go of without a fight... or at least an explanation.

Brody returned with the ball and dropped it at Mason's feet. This time Mason sent it into the tall plants intentionally, using the time to look up into the clear morning sky. He took a couple of deep breaths and cleared his mind. Prayer always centered him. He gave God thanks for a restful night asking for His presence and wisdom and, as always, lifting his son, Garrett, up for protection, thankful that he'd found his way to God years before his old man.

Mason paused and gathered his thoughts.

Father, You've always blessed me, even when I wasn't aware of it. You gave me three decades with a wonderful woman, and I'm more grateful than I have words to express. If it's Your will, I think I'm ready to explore an option for more. I don't know what happened last night, but I know misery when I see it. I saw plenty in Syd's eyes. Would You be with her today? Provide her with the wisdom and direction she needs to work through the problem. Remind her that she has friends she can depend on.

Mason enjoyed another five minutes with his dog before the unpacked boxes started screaming his name in his late wife's voice.

* * *

"This is so not fair." Ginny held the phone to her ear while she paced the yellow-and-white bedroom. It was a nice enough room in a frilly sort of way. There were sheer white curtains at the windows and a pretty comforter on the queen-sized bed. The two doors on the far wall led to a huge closet and a private bath. But pretty didn't change the facts. This wasn't home. It was prison. All that was missing was the orange jumpsuit.

"Gin?"

She took a deep breath and focused back on her boyfriend, Avery. "What?"

"Everything will work out."

The words warmed her and broke her heart at the same time. Avery was such a sweetheart. They'd been a couple for six weeks, and she was pretty sure that he was *the one*. At least he had been until her mother stepped in and ruined everything. Grams could say all day how this was the best solution, but Ginny wasn't buying it, not when it meant leaving her friends and her school behind. Not when it left Grams to take care of Gramps alone. Ginny should be there helping, not exiled to some godforsaken Oklahoma town. She kicked at her suitcase, gratified when the wheels carried it straight into the wall. Nope, this had her mother's fingerprints all over it. Why did her mother have to start caring now? Ginny'd been perfectly happy in Utah for the last eight years. Mom had never made any move to bring her home, not even in the first few months when Ginny'd called every night crying and begging to come home.

"Thanks." Ginny sniffed back tears. "I'm a mess. I don't mean to take it out on you. Can I call you tomorrow?"

"We've got some family thing, and my folks will be ticked if I spend the day on the phone. Can I call you when we're done?"

"Sure. I love you."

"Get some rest."

The phone went dead against her ear, and she let it drop to her side. Avery might not be big on the *I love you* thing, but Ginny knew he cared about her. She opened the bathroom door, yanked off a fistful of toilet tissue, and mopped the tears from her face. She didn't even know which emotion to blame them on.

Anger? Yeah, there was plenty of that. She was mad at Gramps for getting sick, mad at Grams for not needing her help, and Mom? She could write a list.

Hurt? Where should she start? Two days ago, everything had been perfect and then *bam*, her whole world turned inside out.

Fear? Well duh, she was human. No one should have to start over in her senior year. She didn't know anyone in Garfield. Would people like her? Would she like the school? Was there even room for a new kid in all the activities she liked so much? What about a photo club. Did they even have one in this stupid, dinky town?

Maybe she was being a diva. She wouldn't deny it. She was smart enough to know that the world didn't revolve around her, but did the universe have to gang up on her all at once?

Ginny threw herself onto the bed and scooted against the headboard. The motion brought her photo album sliding to her side. She picked it up and thumbed through it. It was filled with pictures from her sophomore and junior photography club field trips. She couldn't help the little smile that tugged at her lips. The pictures on the first pages were so amateurish. The bad lighting and shadowed images literally screamed newbie. But they'd gotten better. The more pages she turned the better the pictures became. She put the book aside and picked up her camera from the bedside table. She hardly went anywhere without it these days. And if she had to be without it, she'd learned to take some amazing pictures with her phone.

A light knock sounded at the door. She removed the lens cap, lifted the camera, and shouted, "What?"

The door cracked open. "Gee, don't take my head off," Sara said.

Ginny took the shot, hoping to capture a look of surprise on her sister's face.

Sara came into the room, closed the door, and leaned against it. She gave her little sister a long, hard stare. "My hair is a mess and my makeup isn't much better. If I see that picture on snapchat, I *will* hurt you."

Ginny thumbed the camera's screen to life and studied the candid shot. All she'd managed to get was the door, but she didn't need to let Sara know that. She gave an exaggerated shudder. "Blackmail worthy for sure."

Sara held out a hand. "Let me see."

Ginny held the camera away. "Let's talk about me borrowing your car."

Sara sent her a look. "I mean it."

The teasing wore thin. Ginny swiped the delete button and set the camera aside. "It's gone." She hunched her shoulders, pulled a pillow into her lap, and buried her face in it. "Just go away." She felt the mattress shift and looked up to see Sara sitting on the foot of the bed, flipping through the photo album.

"No, I don't think so. Mom said you hadn't been out of your room since you guys got home from the airport." Sara lifted an eyebrow. "Sulking?"

Ginny narrowed her eyes. "What if I am?"

"If you are," Sara said, "you need to stop." She tapped a picture of a single yellow flower growing through a split in a boulder. The color of the bloom was brilliant against the blue of the sky and the mottled sheen of the rock. "I like this one." She looked through a few more. "You're really good at this."

"I'm getting there. President of the club this year." She leaned forward and retrieved the book. "Well, I was." Ginny stopped when her voice cracked.

"That's tough." Sara rubbed Ginny's arm. "Talk it out with me. I'm the big sister, I know stuff."

Ginny studied the older girl…woman really, that her sister had become over the last eight years. Resentment bubbled. Sara'd been allowed to stay when Ginny'd been sent away. *And I care about that why? I don't even want to be here.*

"You know you can talk to me," Sara urged.

Ginny snatched her arm from Sara's reach. "Yes, you're the favored one. I'm sure you have all the answers." She pressed her lips together.

Sara's back stiffened. "What?"

"You heard me. Mom always loved you best. She sent me away and kept you close. I didn't like it but I got over it. Excuse me if I'm upset when she turns my life upside-down again."

"You think Mom…" Sara stared at her. "Sent you away…seriously? I can't believe your memory is that selective. After everything Donny did to us, Mom didn't have a lot of choices. Grams and Gramps sued for custody and won because the court in Utah thought our grandparents could offer you more stability than Mom."

"She allowed it, and you got to stay."

The girls stared at each other.

"Look," Sara said. "I was fifteen and pregnant, and I threatened to run away if they tried to take me away from Mom." She got to her feet. "I know it's been hard on you, and I get it that it's even harder now. But you should know something. This is just as hard on Mom."

Ginny straightened. "Then she can send me home."

"That's not what I meant, and I think you know it. I haven't seen Mom this scared in a long time."

"What's she got to be scared of?"

"You."

Ginny crossed her arms and stared at her sister.

"Just you," Sara repeated. "You've grown up without her. She's having a hard time with that. As much as she wanted you home, she wasn't prepared for it. She's been told for eight years that she isn't a good enough mother for you, and she probably believes it." Sara stood and walked to the door. "Get cleaned up and come out to the kitchen. Dinner is almost ready, and Mom cooked all your favorite things. Do us both a favor and try to enjoy the evening."

CHAPTER 3

"Grams and Gramps didn't make me go to church." Ginny crumbled a piece of toast before crossing her arms and slumping back in her chair at breakfast Sunday morning. "Can't I just stay here?"

Syd turned a pancake. *Now there's a thought.* If Ginny didn't come with them this morning, Syd wouldn't have to face the introductions and the questions that would come with them. She could have one more day of normal before she had to start skirting the inevitable explanations.

You're being as childish as your daughter.

"I'm not going to leave you alone on your first morning here."

"I'm seventeen—"

"It's got nothing to do with your age." Syd brought a plate of steaming blueberry pancakes to the table and took a seat across from her daughter. "This is your home now."

"Yippee."

Syd ignored the mumble. "Grace Community has a great group of young people. If you meet some new friends today, maybe you won't feel like such a stranger when we enroll you tomorrow."

Ginny shoved back from the table. "I have friends. In Utah."

Ginny stomped out of the room, brushing by Sara and Logan without a word. Syd's older daughter had spent the night, hoping to ease some of the mother-daughter tension. At least that had been the plan. Though it had failed.

"She's in a good mood," Sara deadpanned.

"We have to give her time." Syd turned her attention to Logan. "I made blueberry pancakes. If Ginny isn't going to eat them, you'll have to double up. You up for the challenge?"

"Yeah, boy!" Logan scrambled for a chair. "Bring 'em."

Sara joined her son at the table and put her arm around his shoulders. "You do know that blueberry is his favorite, right?" She patted Logan's shoulder. "What do you say?"

Logan flinched under her touch. "Ow. You hurt my shoulder."

Sara took a step back. "I barely touched your shoulder."

Logan rubbed the joint. "Still hurts."

Syd set a plate of pancakes in front of her grandson and stooped to his eye level. "Dig in. These will fix you right up."

When he reached for a fork, Syd froze. Under the collar of his pajama top, she saw the edge of a violent purple bruise. She lifted the fabric away and stared in shock at the discoloration covering the whole top of his shoulder. "What has he done to himself?"

Sara turned from the counter, a mug of coffee in her hands. "What?"

"Look at this."

Sara stepped over, put her mug on the table, and bent closer. Her breath whooshed out in a rush as her eyes met her mother's over the top of Logan's head. "Baby, what did you do?"

"Ginny pinched me." The words were a mumble around a mouth full of pancakes.

Sara's eyes hardened. "That brat. I'll—"

"Calm down," Syd said.

"I know she's unhappy," Sara hissed, "but she has no business taking her frustrations out on my son."

"I saw the pinch," Syd said. "You did too. Remember when she got off the plane yesterday?"

Sara pursed her lip as she thought. "That? It was barely a swipe. It shouldn't have caused this."

Logan laid his fork down. "I'm done."

Syd looked at his plate. There were maybe three bites gone. "You sure?"

"Yep."

Sara pulled his chair away from the table. "Go brush your teeth, and get dressed. I'll be there in a second."

"He hardly touched his breakfast," Syd said.

"I know." Sara picked up her coffee and stared down the hall after her son. "I told you his appetite's been weird."

"But you blamed his new video game. No game here, and that bruise isn't right. Maybe you should call his doctor in the morning."

Her daughter's eyes widened. "What do you think is wrong?"

"I don't think anything. It's probably nothing, but better safe than sorry." Syd forked up a bite of Logan's breakfast, chewed, and swallowed. "These are exceptional, if I do say so myself." She pulled the chair out further and shoved Sara into it. "Finish these."

"Where are you going?"

"Gonna go prod your sister. She's not staying home today, and neither am I."

* * *

Pastor Hunter Conklin leaned across the pulpit. "It's been a wonderful morning in the Lord's house. I'm glad each of you decided to worship with us today. Have a great afternoon with your families, and make plans to join us for our evening service tonight at six."

With the pastor's dismissal, the sound of mixing and shuffling filled the auditorium. Women retrieved bags and Bibles. Men moved to the edges of the aisles to have final words with friends they hadn't seen in a week. Young parents hustled from the main sanctuary to pick up their kids from the children's areas.

Syd stood and put an arm around Ginny's shoulder. "That wasn't so bad, was it?"

Ginny shrugged free. "Can we go home now?"

Patience, Syd told herself for the hundredth time in two days. It had taken eight years and the actions of an evil man to destroy what she and Ginny once had. Eight years of regret and prayer lay behind them. Syd hoped that good things lay ahead, but they would each have to get there at their own pace.

"We'll head that way shortly. We're having your favorite for lunch—Crock-Pot chicken and dumplings."

"Can we just stop and get a pizza?"

Patience. And that makes a hundred and one. "Sorry, kiddo. Maybe for dinner tonight after service if you're still in the mood.

"Gee, thanks."

Ginny's sarcasm wasn't lost on her mother, but Syd had bigger issues to deal with right now. Alexandra Conklin, pastor's wife and friend, was headed her way, a welcoming smile on her face. She held a hand out to Ginny as she drew close.

"I was hoping I could catch you. I wanted to welcome you and make sure you knew how much we enjoyed having you with us today. Are you a friend of Sara's?" Her gaze moved from Ginny to Syd, her expression expectant.

Syd opened her mouth to speak, but the words didn't quite clear her throat. She coughed behind her hand and tried a second time. "Alex, this is my younger daughter, Ginny." The flash of confusion on Alex's face was only there for a second. Syd saw it and braced herself for the inevitable questions.

"Well, then, you get more than a handshake." Alex pulled the youngster into a hug and looked at Syd over the girl's shoulder, eyebrows raised. "I sure hope we get to see more of you." She stepped away and pulled Syd into a hug. "Breathe, girlfriend, before you pass out."

The whispered words were barely audible against Syd's ear. She let out a breath and blinked back the tears she was barely keeping in check.

"There you go." Alex gave her a squeeze. "Praying for you."

"Thanks, I need it," Syd answered in her own weak whisper.

Alex took a step away. "I wanted to meet your visitor, but that was only part of the reason I wanted to catch you. I've got something rattling around in my head. God won't let it go, so I'm marshaling the troops for an initial discussion. Are you free Tuesday night? We'll meet at the house about seven. I'll fix something to eat."

"I don't know." Syd glanced at Ginny. "Things are sort of up in the air right now."

"Perfectly understandable. Be there if you can, OK?" Someone called Alex from the front of the church. She sent a final smile to Ginny and Syd. "Never a dull moment on a Sunday morning. Will I see you tonight?"

"I don't think—" Ginny answered.

"Yes," Syd replied at the same time. "Yes," she confirmed. "We're going out for pizza after service. Maybe you could join us. Are the boys home this weekend?" More people at the table, especially Alex and Hunter's handsome twin sons, would ease the tension, wouldn't they?

"They're not." Alex grinned at Ginny. "My twins, Sean and Benjamin. They're sophomores in college this year." Her attention came back to Syd. "They're working some extra hours this weekend. Raincheck?"

"Sure."

"Alex." The summons was more impatient the second time.

"Gotta go."

Syd watched her retreat for a second before turning her

attention to the thinning crowd. She needed to speak to Randy, let her know she'd be late to work in the morning.

"Are we done?" Ginny's question rang with impatience. "I don't want chicken and dumplings, but I'm starving."

Syd muttered a distracted, "Should have eaten breakfast." She spotted her friend and boss, Miranda Page, coming back into the sanctuary with Astor in tow. The four-year-old squealed, "Papa." She broke free from Randy and raced to her grandfather. Grandfather or father? The relationship was confusing. Eli was her grandfather, but he and Randy had adopted the girl almost three years ago, so he was actually both. Syd cut through the row of pews to intercept her redheaded friend.

"Got a minute?"

"Sure, what's up?" Randy asked.

"I need to take a couple hours of personal time in the morning."

Randy's eyes narrowed. "Everything OK?"

"Yes, I ah... I have an errand—"

Ginny cleared her throat.

Syd hadn't realized the girl had followed her. She turned and motioned to the teen, the second introduction no less nerve-racking than the first. "This is my daughter, Ginny. I need to get her enrolled in the morning."

Randy's brows rose over rounded green eyes. "Daugh... I mean, sure. No problem. Take all the time you need. The work isn't going anywhere." She tilted her head, and Syd could almost see a list of questions just behind Randy's eyes. "Will you be at Soeurs?"

"I should have time for a workout before school." She'd make time. She'd gladly pay a year's salary to avoid the questions and explanations that tomorrow held, but she knew from personal experience that questions and explanations wouldn't be the whole of her morning. There would be support and prayer from a group of women who'd become her sisters in the last three years. She needed those things more than breath right now.

Sara came through the main door with Logan. "Thanks," Syd told Randy. "I need to get lunch on the table."

Syd collected her family. She had no doubt that Alex and Randy would share the identity of her young visitor with the others. At least when she walked into the spa in the morning, that part would be done. Now all Syd had to do was decide how little of her eight-year-old tale of humiliation and ignorance she'd be forced to share.

* * *

MASON PUT the bubbling pan of lasagna on a hot pad in the middle of the table. It smelled pretty good for a frozen dinner. He hoped it tasted as good as it smelled because with the addition of a salad and garlic toast it was big enough to feed him three times.

Brody nudged his leg, his canine nose lifted to scent the air. He was tall enough to put his head on the table, but he had better manners.

Mason looked down at the dog and motioned to the corner of the kitchen. "Not on your life, fella. This is mine."

The dog's gaze turned reproachful.

"I should have never given you that first taste of people food when you were a pup. Go lie down."

Brody did as he was told, only going far enough to curl under Mason's chair, sure that his master would relent before the meal was over.

"I don't know which of us is more pathetic."

Mason cut a portion with a spatula, lifting the utensil high as melted cheese trailed from the pan to his plate. He took a tentative taste, and the melted mozzarella pasted itself to the roof of his mouth.

A word he hadn't used in years worked its way up his throat.

31

Mason squelched it, pulled in a gulp of air, and grabbed his glass of iced tea. That was going to blister. He slid the plate to the side to cool and forked up a bite of his fresh-from-the-bag salad.

He chewed and contemplated the day so far. He'd attended church with Garrett and Jesse this morning and was pleased with the welcome he'd received. He'd enjoyed the Sunday school class, Pastor Conklin's message was timely and thought provoking, and several men his age had introduced themselves at the end of the service. He even had an invitation to join in the men's monthly breakfast next Saturday.

But one thing overshadowed all the positives in his experience at Grace Community Church.

Sydney Patterson.

Syd had been five rows in front of him this morning. She'd never looked his way. The one time he'd gotten a good look at her face he'd been taken back by the dark circles under her gorgeous eyes and the tight smile as she spoke to the pastor's wife after service.

He finished the salad, pulled the lasagna close, and took a more cautious bite. "Mmm..." Warm, spicy, and gooey just like he liked it. He'd be buying this brand again.

Brody lifted is head.

"Down boy. You'll have your turn...if you're lucky."

His mind went back to the problem of Syd. After almost forty-eight hours, he was no closer to an answer about what had caused her sudden chill. But there were four things he did know. His mind laid them out in neat order, much like a problem he'd tackle at work.

One: he'd made the move to Garfield for a multitude of reasons. Getting to know Syd was one of them.

Two: he wasn't a quitter.

Three: something had rocked Syd's world on Friday night, and it had nothing to do with him.

Four: He was going to get to the bottom of this. The lady needed a friend and so did he.

He'd learned in business that if you didn't ask the question, the answer was always no. He would ask the questions.

He'd gotten no response from the two messages he'd left on Syd's phone, but he hadn't played his ace yet. He'd bet money that in all the confusion of whatever problem plagued her, she'd forgotten about their plans for Monday night. If she didn't cancel by the end of the day, he'd arrange to drop in on her before she left work tomorrow. After all, she wasn't answering his calls, and he needed to know what she wanted for dinner.

Weak, his conscience told him.

He didn't care. He'd get the answers he needed even if he had to scale a mountain of resistance to get there.

CHAPTER 4

*S*yd sat in her car outside the spa Monday morning. She was the newbie in this group of women, but she knew the drill. Ginny's unexpected arrival introduced a new wrinkle to the fabric of their friendship. The others wouldn't pry or push for more information than she wanted to share, but there would be questions. Ignoring their natural curiosity would only shine a brighter light on issues Syd didn't want to talk about. Besides, a seventeen-year-old daughter she'd never talked about wouldn't be so hard to explain.

Right.

She slumped in the seat. She needed a story, and - even with the whole weekend to prepare - she hadn't been able to come up with a good one.

Just tell them the truth.

She snorted. "Not likely." The unabridged truth wasn't an option for several reasons, but especially two. She would never expose Sara to ridicule, and Syd couldn't bear the thought of her friends knowing what a naïve idiot she'd been.

So, where the truth was foul and an outright lie just as unpalatable, a glossy half-truth would have to do. If she went in there with a smile and circumvented their questions with a ready-made explanation, it would all be over in a matter of minutes, and they could get on with their workout. Syd rehearsed some options in her head until she had something that would, hopefully, satisfy the five women waiting for her in the room at the top of the stairs.

She bounded up the steps, plastered a smile on her face, and entered the workout area. As she'd anticipated, the others were there already, sitting in a semi-circle on the mat-covered floor, expectant expressions on their faces.

"Morning, ladies. Sorry I'm late." Syd allowed her gaze to brush across Alex, Mac, and Charley, looking to gain some support from her friends also dealing with teens. "You guys know how it goes with a teenager. Everything's an emergency."

Alex studied her. "You look like you're feeling better than yesterday."

Syd smiled. "It's been a bumpy couple of days. I have to admit that when my former mother-in-law first called me with the news that Ginny was finally coming home, I was in a bit of a panic." The expressions of her friends morphed from anticipation to inquisitive. "Not that I wasn't thrilled with the news. I've been praying for it for a long time. It just...well, sometimes God still surprises me." She had no intention of leaving the subject open for discussion. Her hopes were to slam the door on this conversation, lock it, and toss the key into a black hole. The best way to get that done was with a few carefully selected tidbits. She took her place on the mats. "Ask your questions."

The five women looked at each other. Randy bundled her thick red hair into a tail at the nape of her neck and leaned forward. "So, she's been with Anthony's parents for..."

"Almost nine years," Syd said.

Charlene Hubbard's cop's eyes narrowed. "That's a long time."

Mackenzie Cooper frowned. "Yeah...I guess we all thought Sara was an only child."

Jessica Saxton didn't say anything. She just dipped her chin and studied Syd over her glasses.

Syd took a deep breath and launched into her prepared story. "When we lost Anthony, I went through a tough time emotionally as well as financially. Anthony's parents offered to take the kids until I had a better handle on things. Sara refused to go, but I thought their offer made sense for Ginny. I wasn't doing her any good, and it seemed unfair to expect Sara to watch out for her. Once I got my grieving under control, I knew I couldn't stay in Utah with all the memories. And I knew I needed to go back to school if I was going to earn a living." She stopped for a breath and risked a glance at her friends. There was no way to know if they were buying this or not.

Syd didn't have to manufacture the moisture in her eyes. The tears were a byproduct of the never-ending shame that trailed her like the stink of week-old garbage. She swallowed and plowed ahead to the end. "It seemed unfair to rip Ginny's world apart a second time, so when Anthony's parents begged me to let her stay with them, I..." Tears spilled down her cheeks. She swallowed. "I let them keep her. Then I felt ashamed of my own weakness, so..."

Alex scooted forward and took Syd's hands. "That's enough."

Charley stood, pulled tissues from a box on top of the small refrigerator in the corner, and returned to crouch in front of Syd. "We've all had those times."

Randy leaned forward to pat Syd's foot. "What's important is that she's with you now."

Syd took the tissue, blotted her eyes, and focused on Jesse.

Jesse's face wrinkled in a frown. "Didn't you tell us you remarried?"

Syd felt as if she'd been punched in the gut. She lifted the tissue and blew her nose in an effort to buy a few seconds while she searched her memory. What had she told them about Donny? They'd only been married for six months, if you could call it a marriage, and she never talked about him. Maybe his name had come up during one of their countless heart to heart talks, but she couldn't remember any details. She took a breath. If they didn't know about Ginny, they didn't know about Donny and Sara and Syd's failures as a parent and a woman.

She'd admit to the marriage and put a quick stop to that line of questioning. "That's a story for another day." She stood and held out her hands. "Would you guys help me pray? Ginny's here because of some health issues with her grandfather. She just started her senior year, and she isn't happy about the move."

"Bless her heart, that's got to be tough. We'll pray for your father-in-law as well." Alex scrambled to her feet and took her hand on the right while the others hurried to stand and close the circle.

"Could I..." Mac paused and glanced at Syd. "I don't mean to intrude on your prayer—"

"Don't be goofy," Syd told her, eager to have the focus shifted away from herself. "What's going on?"

"I just don't feel well." Mac twitched a shoulder. "I think I've picked up a bug or something, or maybe I just need vitamins. I'm tired all the time. Dane thinks I'm already bored with him." Her chuckle lacked any of her normal humor. "We sit down after dinner, and I'm asleep before he gets five words out of his mouth. All I do is eat and sleep." She picked at her T-shirt. "My clothes are getting tight, and I feel like a slug. I almost called you guys to cancel our session this morning because my stomach was upset."

"Aww," Charley said. "Fall in Oklahoma. Changing leaves, renewed bad weather, and fifty different viruses to choose from."

"I hate allergy season." Randy sniffed and dabbed at her nose.

Jesse wiggled a finger between Randy and Mac. "You two need to make doctor's appointments before—"

"Speaking of doctors," Syd interrupted. "Something's up with Logan too. Sara's taking him in for a check this week."

"Well," Alex said. "Looks like God has His work cut out for Him. Let's get Him on it."

Syd watched as one by one the women bowed their heads. She'd been so blessed with this circle of friends.

You lied to them.

She pushed the little niggle of guilt away. She hadn't lied...not really. They didn't need the nuts and bolts of the story to help her pray.

"Father," Alex began. "Thank You so much for loving us. Thanks for giving us a place of peace and safety when the problems of this world get too heavy. Lord, we give You special thanks that You've made a way for Syd's family to be reunited. Watch over Ginny. Help her adjust to her new home, and give Syd the patience and wisdom she needs during this time of transition. We ask for a healing touch for Mac, Randy, and Logan. You created us. You know us better than we know ourselves. Restore each of them to perfect health. We ask these things in the awesome name of Your son, Jesus, and we will give You all the praise. Amen."

* * *

SYD LOVED her job as Randy's administrative assistant. The world of small-town finance fascinated her, and Randy was the best boss in the world. Of course, Syd had no basis for comparison as far as bosses were concerned. She'd gone straight from her parents' home to the home Anthony and she had made without ever having to exercise her associate's degree in office administration. His work as an electrical engineer had provided handsomely for their family and allowed her to be a stay-at-home wife and mother. She'd cherished those years, never giving any thought to the progress being made in the world around her until Anthony died so suddenly.

Oh, she'd learned to use a computer to keep in touch with

friends, keep her household funds in order, and place an order at Amazon. But the computer revolution in the business world had passed Syd by while she'd raised her babies. Once the dust had settled from Donny's betrayal, she knew she needed a serious job, not just to pay the bills but to give her mind something to focus on while she healed. To her surprise, her twenty-year-old degree was useless in the face of a computerized world.

Randy had been a godsend. She'd taken one look at the nervous applicant sitting across from her desk, studied the twenty-year-old degree and the fresh documentation from a vo-tech computer course, and given Syd the job. Six years later they were more than employer and employee, they were friends.

Syd slid into her chair at nine-thirty Monday morning more grateful than ever to have this outlet. The relief she'd found in her friend's acceptance of her sketchy story and the peace of their early morning prayer had evaporated in the face of Ginny's obstinate refusal to accept the changes in her life.

Syd put her elbows on her desk and laid her head in her hands. She wished she could ship the girl back to Utah. Except she didn't, not really.

"Trouble?" Randy asked.

Syd raised her head and let out a slow breath. "Ginny's miserable, and when a teenager ain't happy, ain't nobody happy. I'm depending on you to have enough work to keep my mind focused on other things."

Randy gave her a wicked smile. "Be careful what you ask for." She tapped a stack of envelopes sitting on the corner of Syd's desk. "Delivery guy just brought these. My guess is that they are last week's mortgage loan requests fresh from the approval committee. Now you get to log them in, sort through them, and give me an update. How's that for busy?"

"I love you."

Randy turned back to her office. She flipped a hand in the air.

"Please…" A second later she was back standing in front of Syd's desk. "I've got a meeting with the city council in fifteen minutes."

"And a meeting with the board of trustees right after lunch."

Randy glared at her.

Syd raised her hands in mock surrender. "Don't shoot the messenger."

"Right. Well, I'll see you sometime before five." She headed to the door and paused. "How is Ginny getting home from school? Do you need to leave?"

"Sara's getting her. She's spending the night with Sara and Logan. Thanks for asking, though."

"OK." She waved at the stack of envelopes. "I'll be back in plenty of time to go over this mess."

Syd worked through the rest of the morning, expecting a phone call from the school or Ginny, but her phone remained blessedly quiet. Lunch came and went with barely a pause for a cold sandwich and chips. The stack on her desk dwindled, and the report she compiled for Randy held mostly good news. Of the twenty-eight requests for mortgage funding, only five had been rejected, and of those five it looked as if three only needed additional paperwork.

Randy would handle the delivery of the news to each applicant, but making the appointments was Syd's job. She still found it hard to keep her poker face in place and her voice neutral when she knew the news wasn't what the borrower had hoped for. Scheduling so many positive appointments would be easy.

By the time Syd headed to Randy's office to deliver her report, it was pushing five-thirty. Outside her office in the main lobby of the bank, business had picked up as people rushed to complete their banking before the lobby closed. Inside the inner office, her redheaded boss bundled her thick mane of hair in one hand, leaned her head against the tall back of her seat, and rested her bare feet on the edge of the desk.

Syd made herself comfortable in one of the visitor chairs. "Hard day?"

"I'll live." Without opening her eyes, she continued, "Please tell me that we have more good news than bad this time around."

"It's the best batch we've had in weeks."

Randy lowered her feet and rocked forward. "What do you want? Name it, and if it's in my power, it's yours."

Syd laughed and handed a file folder across the desk. "Twenty-three approvals, three rejections pending additional paperwork, and only two outright dismissals. Where do you want to start?"

They were done in less than thirty minutes. Syd gathered her notes into a folder. "That wasn't so bad, was it?"

Randy beamed. "News like this is one of the reasons I love my job." She motioned to the folder. "Most of those contracts represent first time home buyers. Young families looking to buy a house and turn it into a home. Saying no hurts, but getting to say yes... We get to be a little part of fulfilling their dreams. It makes me happy." Randy glanced at her watch and slipped her feet back into her shoes. "Speaking of happy...I need to get home. Astor is having a little friend over for dinner and a play date. I have chicken nuggets to heat and mac and cheese to make. Yummy."

Syd followed Randy out of the office. "I..." Her words trailed, her feet froze, and heat worked its way up from under her collar as Mason scrambled to his feet. What was he...? The memory of her offer to help him unpack came back in a flash. She watched while he and Randy exchanged pleasantries. He was so stinking handsome. Syd jerked when Mason laughed at something Randy said. Longing filled her. It'd only been two days, and she missed their chats, missed hearing the way his deep voice said her name. That type of longing made you careless. It was exactly the reason she couldn't help him. Not tonight, not ever.

CHAPTER 5

*S*yd stood to the side, her hands clasped behind her back while Randy and Mason finished their brief conversation. Randy glanced at her watch.

"I really have to scoot. It was wonderful to see you again." Her attention shifted to Syd. "Enjoy your evening of peace and quiet. I'll see you in the morning."

Syd frowned at Randy's back as the excuses she'd intended to make to Mason about how busy she was tonight suffered an impromptu death. *Gee, thanks, boss.*

Once they were alone, Mason sent Syd one of his devastating smiles. "I hope you don't mind that I stopped by. I got free earlier than I expected and decided to drop in and clarify what you wanted for dinner."

Syd leaned against the wall, frustration for the situation and affection for the man battling in her heart for dominance. Donny's smiling face flashed through her mind. She straightened and cleared her throat. "I'm afraid Randy misunderstood. I'm going to have to bow out of our plans for this evening."

Mason tilted his head. "Let me guess. You need to wash your hair."

She stared at him.

"You got a new book, and you're dying to read it?" He snapped his fingers. "No, I've got it. You won the lottery, and you have to go claim your prize."

Syd felt the corners of her mouth twitch at his joking. "No."

Mason wiped imaginary sweat from his brow. "That's good, I thought you were serious about ditching me for the evening." His voice lowered and his gaze locked onto hers. "Please, don't be serious."

She looked away, her resolve wavering. There was no room for a man in her life with Ginny home, but she owed Mason more than just an out of pocket dismissal. It couldn't hurt to have a final meal with him, give him the same story she'd told her friends earlier in the day, and say a proper good-bye.

Except it just prolongs the inevitable.

She pushed the little voice aside and pulled in a shaky breath. "I like spring rolls and sesame chicken with noodles instead of rice."

"Some of my favorites." He watched her for a few seconds before crossing the room. He stood close enough to touch her but merely waited until she raised her eyes to his. "You have my address?"

She nodded. "In my purse."

"Good. Get your stuff together and meet me at the house in thirty minutes. We'll have dinner, and you can help me sort out the decorating."

Syd couldn't bear the sincerity in his gaze and turned her face away.

He caught her chin in his hand and prevented the emotional retreat. "We haven't spent a lot of time together, but I thought we were friends."

"We are," she whispered. *Were.*

"Then don't shut me out. You can talk to me about anything,

even what's put that haunted look on your face." He waited just a beat before turning to leave her office.

Syd watched him go, wishing with every fiber of her being that she could believe him.

* * *

MASON CIRCLED THE BLOCK. Garfield wasn't a vast metropolis, but they did have several better-than-average dining options. Thank goodness one of them was Chinese. Really good Chinese as he'd learned from his visit six months ago.

He parked and sat for a couple of minutes. He wasn't an expert where women were concerned, but there was little doubt that Syd was about to bolt.

And not just for the evening.

That was the last thing he wanted. He figured he had tonight to reinforce their friendship.

People hurried by on the sidewalk, rushing in both directions to get their end of day errands completed so they could settle in for the evening. The door to the restaurant opened and closed a half dozen times while Mason sat in the car and thought about the best way to handle the brewing situation with Syd. Nothing came to mind. Finally, he closed his eyes.

"Father, I know that You know what has Syd so upset. I don't need the details, but any insight You could offer me about how to help her would be greatly appreciated." He paused, glancing out the window of his car. The foot traffic continued without a passing glance for the guy sitting in the parked car talking to himself. Mason had only been a Christian for a couple of years, and there were times when prayer still felt a little odd. "I like Syd. Something feels right when we're together." Mason stopped a second time and pulled a hand down the length of his face. Might as well be honest. God knew the facts. "You know I more than like her, but more than what I want, I want Your will for my life and hers."

Be her friend.

The words came out of nowhere, so clearly that Mason jumped, shifted his gaze to the rearview mirror, and then laughed at himself. He gave himself a few seconds for his heart to stop pounding.

Be her friend.

There it was again, quieter and more internalized than the first time. Mason waited a bit longer. When nothing else came, he got out of the car, beeped the locks closed, and entered the restaurant. He had his marching orders.

Twenty minutes later, the aroma of carry out driving his stomach crazy, Mason pulled into his drive. He was a few minutes late and not surprised to see Syd's car parked at the curb. Her door swung open at the same moment as his, and she hurried to his car.

"Sorry I'm late." He climbed out and leaned back in for their dinner. "The place was packed. I got their card. Next time we want Chinese, I'll call it in."

Mason didn't miss Syd's tight smile at his mention of *next time*. He ignored it. There would be a next time…and a next time after that if he had anything to say about it. He motioned to the house. "After you."

Syd eyed the bags suspiciously before she turned toward the house. "What all do you have in there?"

"Oh, this, that, and the other thing. There were five people in front of me. Everything they ordered sounded too tasty to pass up. We'll have plenty, and I can eat the leftovers for a few days."

They stepped up onto the porch, and a muffled bark filtered through the door. "That's Brody." Mason handed some of the bags to Syd and fitted the key in the lock. "I forgot to ask…do you like dogs?"

Before Syd could answer, Mason swung the door wide, and Brody joined them on the porch. He ignored the bags of food and gave his full attention to sniffing Syd's shoes and her outstretched hand. Syd handed the bags back to Mason and crouched in front of the dog.

"Aren't you a handsome guy?" She buried her fingers in the long fur around his ears and scratched. Brody gave a long, low whine of pleasure.

"You keep that up, you're going to have a friend for life."

Syd continued to pet the ecstatic dog. "I don't have a problem with that. A person can't have too many friends."

Mason led the way into the house. That was a really good point. One he'd be duty bound to remind her about if tonight's conversation took the negative turn he expected.

* * *

"GOD BLESS MOMMY and Grandma and Auntie Ginny. Amen."

Logan finished his bedtime prayers and scrambled onto the mattress, leaving his mother to rise at a less hurried pace. He stretched out on the mattress and winced.

"What's wrong, big guy?"

Logan shifted and rubbed his left knee. "Hurts."

Sara looked at the indicated joint in the soft light of the bedside lamp and gave an inward sigh of relief. No discoloration. Not like on his shoulder and a dozen other new places she'd seen while helping him with his bath. Violent, purple bruises that neither she nor Logan had an explanation for. She'd asked if he'd been in a fight on the playground. He denied it, and surely his teacher would've called if there'd been an incident at school.

She pulled the blanket over her son and handed him the bedraggled teddy bear he'd been sleeping with his whole life. "Get some sleep. It'll be better in the morning."

"Tummy too?" Logan's hand moved from his knee to his middle.

Sara closed her eyes at the question. First the bruises and sore joints, now bedtime stomachaches? "That too."

He smiled at her with that look of utter confidence little boys saved just for their moms.

Something inside of Sara twisted. "I'm going to make an appointment for you to see Dr. Joe. See if he can figure what's got you messed up."

"OK." Logan rolled to his side, taking the bear with him, and closed his eyes. His breathing was already leveling out.

Sara sat on the side of the bed for a few minutes listening to her son breathe as he slipped into sleep. Love washed through her with each exhale. Everything good in her life was wrapped up in this seven-year-old package of always ornery, often smelly little boy. How could she have dreamed that God could take such devastation and turn it into a blessing? She leaned down, brushed unruly blond hair from his forehead, and touched her lips to the skin next to his ear.

"I love you," she whispered. Her baby never moved. Sara closed her eyes. *Father, thank You for trusting me with this sweet little life. I love him so much it's scary. Please watch over him while he sleeps. I don't know what's going on with him, but would You touch him, whatever it is?*

She got to her feet, turned the lamp down to its lowest setting, and tiptoed from the room.

"He asleep?" Ginny looked up from where she'd sprawled on the secondhand sofa that dominated Sara's small living room.

"Yep." Sara moved to the far end of the sofa and batted at her sister's sock-covered feet. "Make some space."

Ginny folded the senior English book away and tucked her feet up beneath her so that her sister could sit. "Is he OK? I mean…he barely touched his dinner, and it's sort of early for bed, isn't it?"

Sara studied her. "From your vast parenting experience." Ginny stuck her tongue out and Sara continued. "He is acting a little weird, but I've got the Ps covered."

"Ps?"

"Prayer and Physician. Praying for him every day and making him a doctor's appointment in the morning."

Ginny put her head in her hands. "Not you too."

"Me too what?"

"This whole God thing Mom's got going on. Sounds like she's corrupted you."

"Corrupted?" Sara crossed her arms, but Ginny continued.

"Infected, brainwashed…whatever. It's weird, and I thought you were smarter than that."

"You're the weird one. Don't you believe in God?"

Ginny glanced at the ceiling. "That He's up there? Sure, I guess. That He's the answer to all my problems? That sounds a whole lot like a crutch to me."

"That's all you got from attending church with Grams and Gramps. That God was a crutch?"

Ginny looked at her fingernails. "They didn't make me go. When I was about fifteen, they said I was old enough to start making a few decisions for myself. It's my life, after all. Running to some invisible someone every time things don't go your way, that's silly, but it sounds like something Mom would buy into. She's good at pushing her problems off on others."

"Your cracker has lost its cheese."

Ginny scoffed.

Sara rolled her eyes. "Would you like to borrow some of my marbles 'cause you've lost most of yours."

"Just speaking the truth."

"Your truth isn't very fair."

Ginny made a face. "Easy for you to say since you're the daughter who got to stay."

"I thought we talked this out Saturday night."

Ginny snorted. "Yeah, well, then came Sunday. Her friends didn't even know I existed. What sort of love is that?"

Sara twisted a strand of blonde hair around a finger. *Father, she's got it all wrong. What can I say to her to make her understand?* She looked at Ginny. "When you say it like that, it sounds pretty awful—"

"Ya think?"

"But, I'm to blame, not Mom."

Ginny opened her mouth, but Sara held up a hand.

"Mom didn't keep you a secret because she didn't love you. She did that because she loved me. You weren't here, and you weren't going to be. What Donny did…what I did…" Sara bowed her head, her hair curtained her face, and heat crept up her neck. "Coming to Garfield gave us…me a chance for a fresh start. Mom didn't want me to live with that hanging over my head every day. The easiest way…the hardest way…to prevent that was just keeping quiet about the past. Explaining about you, meant explaining about me. So if you need to be mad at someone, then be mad at me."

Ginny looked down at her lap and twisted the class ring round on her finger. When her head came up there were tears in her eyes. "I guess I get that, but it still hurts."

"I know, but think about it, OK? Mom loves you, and so do I. You've come home. It's a change for all of us, but if we work at it we can be a family again." And that was enough heart to heart for her little sister to chew on for one night. Sara tapped the school book. "Tell me about your first day at Garfield High."

Ginny blinked at the rapid change in subject. "Not much to tell. Of all my new teachers I think I like Mrs. Hall best. I signed up for the school chorus. There's a photo club meeting tomorrow. I hope it's not too late to join.

"Any boys catch your eye?"

Ginny snorted. "I have a boyfriend in Utah."

"Really?" Sara gathered her legs beneath her. "What's his name?"

"Avery."

"And...?" Sara prodded.

Ginny huffed out a breath. "And I'm mad at him right now, so I don't want to talk about him."

"Mad why?"

"Because he promised to call me yesterday, and he didn't. I haven't talked to him today either. Something's wrong, but I'm in stupid Oklahoma not Utah, so I don't know what it is."

"Want some guy advice?"

Ginny raised an eyebrow.

"Don't stress over it, Guys don't think like we do. When he calls, he'll have some perfectly lame reason that he expects you to accept, no questions asked." She held out her hand.

"What?"

"Oh, come on. I know you have a picture on your phone," Sara said. "Take pity on me. I'm a single mom with a job and no time for men."

Ginny rolled her eyes, dug her phone out of her pocket, and thumbed it to life. After a few swipes, she handed it to Sara.

Sara studied the redheaded, bespectacled geek on the small screen. Not her idea of a hunk... "Wow, he's a hottie."

Ginny snatched the phone.

Sara sat back and crossed her arms. They were sisters, but the years of separation and the experience of those years had left them with little common ground. A sudden thought made her smile. "I have Scrabble."

"Really?"

Sara untangled her legs, pushed herself off the sofa, and crossed to a small closet. She opened the door and rummaged for a few moments before turning back with the game in her hand. "Never been opened."

Ginny shoved to her feet, marched past her older sister, and settled at the kitchen table. "Bring it."

"Gladly," Sara responded. "I'll be looking for a seven letter word that means brat."

CHAPTER 6

*S*yd leaned back in her chair and dabbed at her mouth with a brown paper napkin emblazoned with the name of Garfield's one and only Chinese restaurant. No fewer than ten boxes of food sat open and scattered across the table. The meal had been much more than the sesame chicken and noodles she'd requested. And even though her mouth still stung from a single bite of something Mason had called *Er kuai* spicy chicken, the meal had been pleasant in every way. But the time for pleasant was over. As much as she hated it, she needed to initiate a conversation and put an end to the fantasy she'd begun to build around Mason Saxton.

"I need—" she began.

"We need—" He spoke at the same time, then made a motion with his hand. "Sorry. Ladies first."

"Thanks." Syd swallowed, and everything she'd primed herself to say disappeared in the glow of Mason's smile. *Get it over with, for both your sakes.* She leaned forward, determined to yank the Band-Aid off this sore spot in one quick, merciful pull.

"I want you to know what a lovely time I've had getting to know you. You're an amazing man, and under other circumstances, nothing would make me happier than getting to know you better." Syd's throat closed in a vice of useless emotion. She reached for her glass of iced tea and took a deep drink. What was wrong with her? She was fifty years old and self-sufficient. Hadn't she moved beyond the trivial idea of needing a man to make her life complete? Hadn't Donny's betrayal been the last straw on that issue?

Yes, something in her wounded heart screamed. *That lesson cost dearly, and we don't need to repeat it.*

No, something deeper whimpered. The something deeper was the part of her that wanted to take long hand-in-hand walks in the snow with a man who loved her. The part of her that longed for quiet evenings at home with that man, sharing popcorn and laughter while they watched TV. The part that dreamed of whispered conversations in the dark before falling asleep and waking up next to that man. The part of her that remembered how much easier the burden of everyday life became when shared with a man who cared.

You're a fool to go there, the wounded part yelled, burying the *something deeper* in memories of hurt, betrayal, and shame that Syd refused to bring into the light.

While the battle raged, Mason sat across from her and waited in silence, his expression attentive, his eyes tender.

Something turned over in Syd's heart. Not some nebulous idea of a man she conceded. *This man.* The blinding moment of clarity propelled her out of her seat and sent her pacing the length of the room. Tears stung the backs of her eyes, and she pushed them back ruthlessly. *Father, give me strength not to be stupid again.*

She faced him. "I'm sure that you've heard that my youngest daughter has come to live with me."

"Jesse told me. Was that the phone call that upset you on Friday night?"

"Yes…not upset though, just…" Her voice cracked, and despite her resolve a tear spilled down her cheek. "Surprised."

Mason stood, took a step toward her. "Hon…"

Syd stopped him with a raised hand. "I'm OK." She swiped the moisture away with the crumpled napkin. "Ginny and I have been separated for a long time." She fed him the rest of her practiced story in a rush, the same scanty details and half-truths she'd shared with her workout partners earlier. It didn't taste any better the second time around, but it was for everyone's protection, Ginny's, Sara's, and hers. "We need some space to put our relationship back on track. That's where my time and attention need to be right now. I know you can understand that."

Mason rocked back on his heels, pursed his lips, and looked up at the ceiling. She could almost see the cogs turning in his head as he worked through what she'd said. When his chin lowered and his gaze met hers, he said, "Of course I understand. Your girlfriends must be horribly devastated."

"My girlfriends?"

"All those amazing women I met a few months ago. My daughter-in-law, Jesse, Alex, Mac, Charley. Even your boss, Randy. They must be distraught over your decision."

Syd tilted her head. "I'm not sure what you mean."

"Your absence will leave a horrible void in their lives." Mason turned to the table and began to close up the boxes of takeout. "If I'm hearing you correctly, you're telling me that you need to spend all of your spare time with Ginny. That until you get your relationship with your daughter 'back on track.' you don't have time for friendships, mine or theirs. And for Ginny to enter into such an agreement is nothing less that extraordinary. The knowledge that she's willing to forego new friends and activities, in her senior year, in a new school, in favor of spending all her spare time with you must soothe your heart."

Syd knew her expression was more than a little confused. "I don't think… I mean Ginny isn't…"

Mason looked up from the table, eyebrows lifted.

"I'd never ask Ginny to put off making friends. I want her to have friends."

"Does she want the same for you?"

Syd exhaled heavily. "Why wouldn't she?" Her mouth snapped shut as she realized the carefully laid trap she'd just stumbled into.

His expression saddened. "I see. It's not friendships you plan to avoid, it's just me."

Syd clasped her hands at her waist and picked at her nails. "I can't..." She stopped and tried to gather her scattered thoughts. *Be careful*, a little voice warned, *too much information is a bad thing.*

MASON HAD HER. He hated the underhanded tactics, but he wasn't going to let her out of his house, or his life, as easily as she seemed to think. He didn't flinch when Syd glared at him.

"You completely twisted my explanation."

He concentrated on stacking the containers on the counter. There was so much missing from her *explanation* it barely qualified for the name. He itched to peel back the layers, to get to the core of the problem, to fix what had hurt her. And he had no doubt that hurt was the correct word. When he faced her again, her shuttered expression and flat eyes only verified his intuition.

Be her friend.

There it was again. That quiet admonition. Mason sent up a quick prayer. *I hear You. This isn't a one-sided decision though. I need some direction.*

He turned to face her and shrugged. "I'm a guy, but I'm not clueless. A blind man could see that you're scared to death right now. You've been teetering on the raw edge of panic ever since your phone rang Friday night. I might not know the cause—"

"You—"

"And I don't need to." He crossed to where she stood and took her hands in his. They were ice cold and trembling. He raised them, tucked them under his chin, and looked down at her. "What I need to do...what I want to do, is be your friend. I know you need time with your daughter, but Ginny is going to be busy with her friends and schoolwork. All I'm asking is that you share some of that leftover time with me."

Syd squeezed his hands, pulled hers gently from his grasp, and tucked them behind her back before leaning against the wall. Mason took a step back to give her some additional space. He didn't want her to feel trapped.

He continued, "Despite all the long distance calls and late night chats, we're just getting to know each other. I don't want that to end. I want to get to know the woman I've come to admire. I promise I won't pry into things you don't want to share, but I want to help you through a difficult time. It's what friends do. It's biblical."

Syd stared up at him. "Is that so?"

"There's a verse—don't ask me where—but it talks about sharing a burden. I can look it up for you if you have time."

Her lips tipped up. "Galatians six-two."

"Maybe..."

"'Bear ye one another's burdens and so fulfil the law of Christ.'"

Her words were barely a whisper. Mason took heart from the fact that she hadn't bolted from the room. "That's it." He paused, trying to tread lightly around the things she wasn't telling him. "I know you're worried about the drastic turn your life took this weekend. I've got pretty broad shoulders. Will you let me carry some of that burden for you?"

A small smile trembled at the corners of Syd's mouth, a sign of warmth that might have encouraged Mason if it had reached her eyes. Instead, the deep brown of her gaze shifted to a point over his right shoulder and glistened with unshed tears.

* * *

HE QUOTED SCRIPTURE TO ME. Syd wanted to believe that made Mason one of the good guys. He wanted to be her friend, to spend time with her, and share her problems. She wanted to believe that there were no ulterior motives, that what he said was the truth, but her daughters had suffered for her foolishness so much already.

Really. The little voice in her head mocked her. *He quoted scripture to you? And that makes his motives pure? The devil knows scripture. Didn't you learn anything eight years ago?* Syd closed her eyes against the memories that flooded her heart and mind.

The room had been dark except for the flicker of the movie on the TV screen. They'd been watching Ghost, *Donny on the couch beside Syd, the girls sprawled on the living room floor with a bowl of popcorn between them. A homey picture worthy of a Hallmark card. As the characters danced around their apartment, Donny took Syd's hand in his and leaned in to whisper in her ear.*

"Sydney, you're so incredibly beautiful. I could spend my whole life with you and die a happy man."

His lips brushed her ear and ignited a delicious heat that spread down from the side of her face and up from their joined hands and met someplace in her chest. Her heart thudded with an anticipation she hadn't felt since Anthony died. She was grateful for the dark that hid the resulting blush.

"I know your life hasn't been the same since you lost Anthony. I could never take his place... I wouldn't want to try, but I think we could be good together if you'd give us a chance. I want to be so much more than just your friend, Syd. Will you think about it?"

Oh, she'd done more than just think about it. She'd allowed herself to be swept away by ideas of love and second chances, flattered and grateful that a handsome man ten years her junior would want her.

And her daughters had paid the price.

And here she was again. Eight years older, flattered by another man, longing for things she couldn't have, seemingly oblivious to the lessons life and Donny had taught her.

Syd's eyes snapped open, and she struggled to pull air into her lungs. How long had she been standing there, frozen in time and space while her stupidity replayed in her head? Mason stood right where he'd been, watching her with confusion etched onto his face.

Tell him the truth.

To what end? He'd certainly walk away if he knew the truth, and even if he didn't, she didn't want his pity. Syd took a step forward, raised up on her toes and brushed his cheek with a kiss. "You're a good man, Mason. I wish things could be different." She grabbed her bag from where it hung on the back of her chair and bolted out of the house without a single backward glance.

"Syd!"

She kept walking even though the ache in her heart was enough to cripple her.

She took her time on the drive home, ignoring several incoming texts on her phone, torn by conflicting emotions and confused by the two voices arguing in her heart. She'd done it. She'd walked away from a dangerous situation. Shouldn't there be some relief in that?

Syd unlocked the door to her house, stepped into the softly lit entryway, leaned against the door as it closed, and let the tears fall. She'd done the right thing, hadn't she? Her phone beeped again and she looked at it.

Mason.

I'm sorry if I said something wrong. Please let me know that you made it safely home.

Her hand dropped to her side, and she bowed her head.

Jesus, You blessed me before I knew You with Anthony and the life we built. When that life crashed, I was so lost. When Donny came into my life, I was still grieving, and he looked like the answer to prayers I hadn't even prayed. She blew out a breath and refused to examine the memories too closely. *But that's the past, sins You've forgiven me for. Sins I don't want to repeat. I've worked so hard to build a life here, to make a home for Sara and Logan. You've filled my life with good friends. Now You've brought Ginny home, and as unhappy as she is right now, I know things are going to work out because I've given You control. Those blessings merit a little caution, don't they?*

Syd pushed away from the door. It was just past eight, but she wanted sleep and the oblivion it brought. She undressed in the dark, checked to make sure her alarm was set, and crawled between the sheets. The tears continued as she lay, looking at the ceiling, lulled by the turning blades of the ceiling fan. *Anthony... Donny...Mason...* She bit her lip to keep it from trembling. *I'm so confused. Please give me the strength and clarity of mind to know what You want me to do.* Comfort as if arms had wrapped around her filled her heart, and she relaxed into it. She slept with those final words of prayer ringing in her mind. *Please help me know what You want me to do.*

CHAPTER 7

Sara was the perfect picture of a frazzled young mother on Tuesday morning. Up early to call her supervisor to let him know that she'd be late because Logan needed to see his doctor. No, she didn't know how long it would take. Yes, she would let him know about her adjusted arrival time just as soon as she could. That done, she'd hustled Ginny and Logan out of bed, and enlisted her little sister's help with the morning battle. Logan was the joy of Sara's life, but he was not a morning person, always crabby and slow to function. Sara had wondered, often, if allowing a seven-year-old a cup of coffee to help clear the cobwebs would make her a bad mother. This morning she was grateful to have Ginny there to deal with part of it.

She served a breakfast of scrambled eggs, toast, juice, and milk—chocolate for Logan—at seven, dishing food with one hand, the other holding the phone glued to the side of her head while terminal hold music played in her ear.

"Good morning. How may we help you?"

Finally. "This is Sara Marlin. I need to bring Logan in to see Dr. Joe."

"I'm sorry this is his answering service. The office won't open for another hour."

Sara closed her eyes and tapped the phone against her forehead. She knew that.

"We can take your number and have the receptionist call once the clinic opens."

"Fine." Sara gave them the number. "Please make sure they get it. It's important."

"Of course. The twenty-four-hour clinic is an option as well as the ER if you think it's an emergency."

"Thanks." Sara dropped the phone and called down the hall. "Breakfast is ready, guys. Get a move on. We need to leave in less than an hour."

Logan limped into the kitchen, favoring his left leg. She bent down to give him a hug. "How you doing, buddy?"

"I don't feel good, Mommy."

"I know." She held up the phone. "I've got a call in to Dr. Joe."

Logan brightened. "And Miss Sadie?"

The question made Sara smile. "And Miss Sadie." She took a seat next to her son as a bleary-eyed Ginny stumbled into the room. "Morning, sunshine."

"Coffee." The word was barely a grunt.

Sara pointed to the counter and sat to enjoy breakfast with her family. Two bites in, Logan shoved back from the table and sprinted for the bathroom. He almost made it before the contents of his stomach erupted in a violent mess.

He sank to his knees at the edge of the disgusting puddle. "I'm sorry, Mommy. I tried to hurry."

Sara battled with her own breakfast as she helped him to his feet and into the bathroom. "I know, baby. Are you better now?"

Logan rubbed his stomach. "Still hurts."

She helped her son out of his ruined clothes and led him to his room, where she laid out fresh jeans and a clean shirt. "Put these on and lie down. I need to talk to Aunt Ginny." *And clean up the mess in the hall.* What a way to start the morning.

Sara buckled Logan into the back seat of her car at eight o'clock and handed him a small plastic lined trash can, just in case. They had fifteen minutes to get Ginny to the high school, and she was still waiting for the clinic to call. She struggled to decide on the best course of action. She didn't know anything about the doctors at the twenty-four hour clinic and emergency rooms were intended for the broken and bleeding, weren't they? Upset stomach, bruises, and tender joints. Sara had dealt with these on an individual basis many times over the years. What mother of an active seven-year-old boy hadn't? But all together? She was in way over her head.

Ginny slouched into the passenger seat just as the phone rang. Sara glanced at the screen. Thank God it was the clinic. "Hello."

"Good morning, this is Dr. Hernandez's office. We had a message to call."

"Yes, thank you. I need to bring Logan in to see Dr. Joe."

"What seems to be Logan's problem?"

Sara started the car. "Can you hang on just a second?" She connected the ear piece and backed out of her parking space before continuing. "Lots of little things. I'm not even sure they're related. He's complaining of joint pain. He bruises if you look at him, and he's lost his appetite. It's probably just some little-boy thing, but I'd feel better if Dr. Joe took a look."

"Hold on while I check his schedule."

"Sure." Music filled her ear as she pulled out on to the street.

The music cut off. "Ms. Marlin, I don't have an open appointment until Thursday. Will that work?"

"I was hoping to bring him in today."

"There's a nasty bug going around."

Sara frowned. A nasty bug that had obviously bitten her son. Her shoulders slumped. "Thursday's fine, but could you call me if anything opens up sooner?"

"We can do that. I'll schedule him in at one on Thursday afternoon and put you on the cancellation call list. The good news is you called early, so your name is at the top."

"Thanks." Sara disconnected. She'd need to let her boss know about the change in plans. She'd only been at her job for five months and was still considered a probationary employee. A late morning today and time off on Thursday wouldn't be in her favor, but Logan came first.

They pulled into the sweeping drive of Garfield High and fell into line with other people dropping off students. Ginny'd remained silent during the drive, either from dread at facing her second day in a new place or respect for Sara's musing. Either way, Sara appreciated the space.

"Mommy?"

Sara looked at Logan in the rearview mirror. Her son's eyes were wide in desperation.

"What is it, baby?" She knew the answer even before he buried his head in the bucket and heaved.

"I'm sorry, Ginny…"

Her sister slid her books onto the floorboard and released her seatbelt. "I'm on it." She twisted in the seat until she was on her knees, steadied the can with one hand, and stroked the boy's hair with the other. "Hang in there, sport, we're right here."

Sara inched the car into place next to the curb, shifted into park, and joined her son in the backseat. Horns honked, people yelled, and Sara ignored them. Once the episode passed, she fished in the pouch on the back of the driver's seat and found a flat packet of baby wipes among the coloring books and toy soldiers. She pulled two or three free and wiped her son's face and mouth. "Better?"

He nodded and leaned back against the seat. His face was pale, and little beads of sweat dotted his forehead and upper lip. The decision became clear. Waiting until Thursday wasn't an option, this was a chore for the ER. Sara glanced up at Ginny, who was still twisted around in her seat, and motioned to the driver's seat. "I need to sit with him for a few minutes. Find us a parking spot, will you?"

Ginny slipped out of the car and sat behind the wheel. She nosed back into the flow of traffic, drove up and down a couple of rows, and finally turned into a vacant spot. Her eyes met Sara's in the mirror. "Is he OK?"

"For now, I think." She held a hand over Ginny's right shoulder. "Will you help me pray for him before you go inside?"

"Sara, I—"

"I'm not interested in your personal beliefs right now, I'm scared, and I need your help. The Bible says that two prayers are better than one. We both want Logan better, and God hears every prayer regardless of the source. Just, ask from your heart." The last words came out choked by tears.

Ginny took her hand. "OK." She bowed her head and closed her eyes.

"Father, please," Sara began, "You see us here. I need direction, and You have the answer. Please help me make the best decision for my son. I—"

Sara's phone rang from the console between the front seats. She leaned forward and snatched it up. Dr. Joe's office. "Hello?"

"Hello, Ms. Marlin?"

"Yes."

"You asked us to call if we had a cancellation. Can you have Logan here by eight forty-five?"

Sara pulled the phone away from her head and looked at the time. Eight-ten. The clinic was twenty miles away in the next town on a road likely to be jammed with morning traffic, not counting unpredictable stoplights and blinking school zones. She ran the route in her head. It'd be close, but the call was an answer to prayer. "We'll be there." She swiped the call closed, patted Logan's back, and grinned at her sister. "Told you God would hear us."

Ginny snorted as she climbed out of the car. "Coincidence, luck…"

"You believe what you want. I'll believe what I know." Sara gave her sister a hurried hug. "We've got to scoot, and you need to get inside before your first class starts."

* * *

Sara signed in at the appointment desk a few minutes early, handed over her debit card for the copay, and hurried Logan around to the pediatric office. They passed the clinic lab on the way. Sara paused when she heard her name. She looked around and saw Mom's friend Mac waving from her seat on the bench outside the lab.

"Everything OK?"

"They've been better." Sara laid a hand on Logan's shoulder. "He's not feeling well."

"Your mom mentioned that. We've all been praying for him —and you."

"I appreciate that." Sara motioned to the lab. "You aren't sick too, are you?"

"No, I think I'm just run down. Dr. Bastille ordered some blood work. I'm sure it's nothing some vitamins won't cure."

Sara glanced at the clock. She had about sixty seconds to spare. "I've got to run. Good luck with your tests."

"You too," Mac settled back on the bench with her magazine.

Sara checked in with the receptionist, found a seat along the wall of the large waiting room, and didn't object when Logan climbed into her lap. She wrapped him close, tucked his head under her chin, and settled in to wait.

A handful of minutes later, a door across the room opened and a pretty nurse dressed in smiley-face scrubs smiled in their direction. "Logan Marlin."

Logan scrambled from Sara's lap. "Hi, Miss Sadie." He took

Sara's hand and tugged her in the direction of the door. "It's our turn."

Dr. Joe and Nurse Sadie had been a part of Logan's life since the day he was born. Dr. Joe worked hard to be a friend to his kids as well as a doctor, and Sara knew her son had a crush on the pretty blonde nurse. That fact worked in everyone's favor when the needles came out and Logan had to make a choice between pitching a fit or manning up to impress Sadie.

Sadie led them to an exam room and patted a paper covered table. "Hop up here, Logan. Let's take your temperature and check out your lungs while Mom tells us what's been going on."

Sara related the list of symptoms. She pulled up Logan's shirt and showed the bruises dotting his back and torso, finishing with the swollen knee and the morning's incident in the car.

"If it was just one or two of these, I wouldn't be so worried, but it seems like he comes up with something new every day." She patted Logan's leg. "We know Dr. Joe will get to the bottom of it."

Sadie typed some notes into the computer that rested on a wall bracket. "I'll get him in here just as soon as I can. Y'all take it easy." She signed out of the computer and left the room, closing the door behind her.

Logan watched her go. "She's the prettiest."

"Buddy, you're about eight years too young to be thinking that way," Sara said.

The paper on the table crackled as Logan leaned back and stretched out. He put his hands behind his head. "I'm going to marry her when I get big enough."

Sara hid a smile behind her hand. She knew Sadie had a husband and two kids of her own. Somehow she didn't think Logan would appreciate her sharing that just now.

A knock sounded at the door, and when it cracked open, a hand puppet in the shape of a gorilla peeked around the edge. *"Es mi amigo Logan aqui?"*

Logan scrambled to sit up. Dr. Joe's last name was Hernandez. He liked to play games with the kids in Spanish. He gave extra lollipops if the kids got it right. "That's me. I am your friend Logan."

A bear of a man edged around the door with the puppet dangling at his side. A wide white smile gleamed against the dark complexion of his face. "Good one. What did I ask you?"

Logan pursed his lips. "Is my friend Logan..." He shook his head. "I didn't understand the last word."

Dr. Joe handed Logan a sucker. "You got most of it. *Aqui* is a new word. It means here. Is my friend Logan here?" He twirled a second sucker. "Extra points if you can say it."

"Es mi amigo Logan...aqui?" The little boy beamed with pride and held out his hand.

"Points for you," Dr. Joe chuckled. He handed Logan the extra candy and turned his attention to Sara. "This is a smart kid. Tell me what's going on."

Sara smiled at the praise and filled the doctor in on the various symptoms. "It was easy to find reasons for the lack of enthusiasm, even the muscle complaints...at least for a few days. But when you add them all up..."

"I understand." The doctor put a hand on Logan's shoulder. "Let's get your shirt off and take a look at some of these bruises." Logan complied, and the doctor raised his brows. "Looks like you went ten rounds with the class bully." He studied Logan's face intently. "Fighting at school?"

"No, sir," Logan answered.

Dr. Joe nodded. "Lie back for me." He touched the bruises with gentle hands, prodding slightly all the way up Logan's torso. He paused for a second at Logan's ribcage when the boy gave a slight wince. "That hurt?"

"A little."

"Hmm." Dr. Joe's fingers continued their exploration up both sides of Logan's neck.

Sara caught the small frown. "What?"

He didn't answer. Instead he held out a hand to Logan and helped him sit up before tossing the boy's shirt over his head. While Logan wrestled with his shirt, the doctor faced Sara. "His lymph nodes are a bit enlarged, so is his spleen." He held up a hand when her mouth came open. "It's not time to panic. I can give you a list of things that cause those particular symptoms, and most are pretty harmless. But...the bruising concerns me. I think we should run some tests."

"What sort of tests? What do you think it is?" Sara's voice quivered on the question.

His expression turned speculative. "Has he been around anyone who might've exposed him to mononucleosis?"

Sara straightened. "Mono? No...I mean...I don't think so. You think that could be it?"

"I'm not ruling anything out just yet. Has he had a fever or a sore throat over the last couple of weeks?"

"Not that he's complained of."

"And he hasn't been around anyone who's been sick over the last seven or eight weeks?"

"No." Sara bit her lip. They'd been to Six Flags and Sea World. Standing shoulder to hip in lines that contained plenty of coughing and sneezing kids and adults, holding onto handrails swiped with God knew what. Had they brought more than matching baseball caps home from vacation?

"Sara?"

She shared her fears with Dr. Joe.

He leaned against the counter. "The timing is certainly right, and those enclosed spaces are ripe for spreading all sorts of infections. We'll draw some blood, do a monospot. I'd bet money that his platelet count is low, which would explain the bruising."

"The nausea?"

"Not a normal symptom, but there's a nasty virus going around. If his immune system is suppressed, he's an unlucky candidate for a double whammy. I'll give him something for the tummy issues. A children's analgesic should help the joint pain."

"How long before we know what's going on?"

"Day or two. In the meantime, keep him home from school. We'll call once we get the blood tests back." He faced Logan. "I'm going to send Nurse Sadie back in to help draw some blood. Tough guy like you won't give her any problems, right?"

Logan swallowed, looked at his mom, and back to the doctor. "A needle?" he asked in a whisper.

Dr. Joe nodded and walked to the door. He opened it and spoke to someone on the other side before turning back to Logan. He held up two fingers about an inch apart. "Just a little one."

A light knock sounded on the door, and Sadie entered.

Logan straightened. "No, sir."

"Tell you what. I'm going to leave another sucker at the front desk. It's yours if you make it through the lab work. But..." He put his hands on his hips. "They'll give it to your mom. You already have two for later. She can save the third for tomorrow. Deal?"

"Deal."

He held out a hand. "Let's shake on it." They sealed the deal in a manly fashion, and the doctor turned to leave. He looked at Sara. "I'll call you."

"Thanks, Dr. Joe."

When he left, a technician from the lab came in. Another pretty young woman, this one of Asian descent with raven black hair and delicate features. Sara almost felt sorry for Logan with the way they were ganging up on him.

The new addition held out a hand. "I am Linn Yie. You are Logan?" Her question filled the room with a lilting accent.

Logan grinned before taking her hand. "Uh-huh. Your words are pretty."

Linn Yie smiled back at him. "Thank you." She carried a tray,

69

which she set on the exam table next to the boy. She selected a few items and looked at Sara. "Have we ever had blood drawn?"

"Not since he was a baby," Sara answered.

"Very well." She turned back to Logan. "I will take time to explain. I think it is more comfortable if you know what to expect." She took Logan's hand and ran her fingers along the inside of his arm, tracing the faint blue lines. "Do you see these lines?"

Logan bent his head to examine what she pointed to. "Uh huh."

"These are veins. Veins carry your blood from your heart to your arms and legs. The blood can tell us many things about you. To get to the story of Logan, we will need to take some out."

"With a needle?" Logan's question held more than a little anxiety despite the company in the room.

"Yes." Linn picked up a small package, ripped it open, and showed it to Logan. "I will use a needle like this. See that it is very small and very sharp. It is sharp so that it hurts less." She retrieved a rubber strap and passed it to Logan for examination. "This will go around your arm. It will be tight, but it will not hurt. It is a magic strap. Once you wear it, the veins in your arm will become easier for me to see." She took the strap back and held up three empty tubes. "I will put your blood in these."

"That's a lot," Logan said.

"Not so much for a big strong boy like you," Linn assured him. "Are you ready?"

Logan looked from his mom to Sadie and back to Linn. He didn't answer but watched closely as the lab tech tightened the strap around his upper arm.

Nurse Sadie stepped to the other side of the table and took Logan's free hand. "Look at me, Logan."

Logan did as she asked.

Linn said, "Sadie is my very talented magical assistant. You must do exactly as she says."

Sara watched as Sadie gave Logan her most brilliant smile. "Does Mama read you stories?"

"We read one about a shepherd and a giant."

"Oh, that sounds like a great story. Can you tell me about it?"

Linn ripped a new needle open, and Logan started to turn toward it.

"Look at me," Sadie told him and tapped her nose with a finger. "Look right at my nose and tell me the story."

"Well," Logan began, his voice hesitant. "There was this little boy named David. He liked to go out into the field and sing God songs to his daddy's sheep. Once a bear and once a lion came to snatch a sheep for their dinner, but David prayed and God helped him save the baby lambs."

Sadie's eyes went round. "Wow. What happened then?"

"David had a ton of bigger brothers. I don't think they liked David very much because they always made fun of him." Logan's voice gained confidence as he got into the story. "But one day when the king called all the brothers to come fight in the war, David's father told him to take some cheese and crackers to them. When David got there, all the guys were hiding behind these big rocks while a hairy old giant stood in the field and made fun of them. David got real mad."

"Mad why?" Sadie asked.

Logan's face scrunched up in thought. "Well, the giant called David's brothers some really bad names. And he called God some really bad names, too." He looked at Sadie. "He was kind of a stupid giant. I guess you can bully brothers, but I don't think God liked it much."

"I don't imagine He did."

"Anyway. David gave his brothers their snack, and he went out to get a drink at the river. While he was there he picked up some rocks and, I think, maybe a frog."

Sadie glanced at Sara with a barely concealed smile. "Oh, I know this story," Sadie said. "The rocks and the frog were magic.

The rocks made David strong, and when David kissed the frog he turned into a super hero."

Logan snorted. "No, girls are so silly. There aren't magic frogs in the Bible. But he did get a good idea. He put the rocks in his bag and went to tell his brothers that he would take care of the giant bully. He waited until the next morning, and when the giant came out and started acting all big and stuff. David put a rock in his slingshot, prayed for God to make it work, and then he shot it at the giant. The giant fell down dead, and the whole army cheered so loud the ground shook."

"All done," Linn said.

Sara grinned, somewhere between magic frogs and dead giants, the blood had been collected, and if Logan felt it, he never flinched. She hoped she could be as brave while they waited for test results.

CHAPTER 8

By lunchtime Tuesday afternoon, Syd was ready to flee the noise of constantly ringing phones and Randy's sunny chatter as she came and went from the office. Syd needed a bit of peace and quiet. Not only was the situation with Mason weighing on her mind, but Sara's report from Logan's doctor… make that a lack of report, since the lab results wouldn't come back for a day or two…had her irritable and in need of a break.

She was waiting for God to give her some direction where Mason was concerned. As for Logan, he was a little boy subject to a host of little boy bumps and bruises. She was trying to be optimistic about the outcome of both. The only problem was that most of her attempts at optimism since Anthony's death had sent her face first into the mud of reality.

She took a quick walk down Garfield's busy little main street, popped into Ground Zero, and ordered a sandwich and chips to go. With the white takeout bag in one hand and a large diet soda in the other, she started back to the bank at a more leisurely pace. Her desk was the ultimate goal, but she wanted to give Randy time to leave for her own lunch so Syd could have a few minutes to herself.

She sipped her drink, pausing in front of Bing's Jewelry and their dazzling array of colorful gems. She wasn't in the market for a new bauble, but what woman could resist the fun of looking? Sweet Moments Bakery and the owner's drool worthy arrangement of baked goods stopped her next. Syd considered a cookie to go with her lunch. One look through the window at the long line at the counter persuaded her not to go inside.

At M and M's Books and Gifts, Syd killed some time in front of the display of new fall releases. She saw a couple of covers that intrigued her and made a mental note to look them up later. Movement just inside the store had her hustling forward to open the heavy glass door for a blonde woman with a baby on her hip. She had one hand holding the hand of a little boy, the other holding a bag of books.

Kate Black stepped out and smiled her gratitude. "Thanks, Syd." She leaned forward to kiss the air next to Syd's cheek. "I haven't seen you in forever. Randy let you out of your cave?"

Syd grinned at her friend. "I manage to escape every once in a while." She hefted the sack of food. "I'm on my way back. I was in the mood for chicken salad, and Ground Zero makes the best."

"That's a fact. How's life treating you?"

Now there's a loaded question. Syd dredged up a smile, prayed that it looked more genuine than it felt, and answered, "Peachy." The baby in Kate's arms began to fuss, and Syd took the opportunity to change the subject. "Looks like you have your hands full today. Babysitting?"

Kate slid the bag of books onto her wrist and offered the baby a pacifier. "On the way to the park for a picnic with the munchkins. Micha, my brother-in-law, was holding a couple of books for me, so we stopped here first."

Syd studied her friend's grandkids, both with dark hair and blue eyes. "They're getting too big, too fast. How old are they now?"

Kate nuzzled the baby's soft cheek with a kiss. "Robin just turned six months, and Chad will be five in a few weeks."

"You have three grandkids, right?"

"Right. Bobbie is the oldest. She's eight and in school today." Kate laughed. "She won't be happy that we snuck out without her, but I'll make it up to her."

The little boy tugged at Kate's hand. "Grandma, I want to go play."

Kate smiled down at him before looking back to Syd. "Duty calls."

The clock at city hall bonged the half hour and reminded Syd of her plan to spend a few minutes alone. "I need to get going too. You guys have a good time at the park." She lifted her face and allowed the September sun to bathe her face in warmth. "You picked a good day for it."

They turned to go their separate ways, but Syd stopped when Kate spoke again.

"Hey, I almost forgot. Do you know anyone looking for a part-time job?"

Syd tilted her head. "Who needs help?"

Kate motioned to the book store. "Micha says they're looking for someone to work two or three evenings a week. Maggie's youngest is in college now, and they need a gopher. My word, not theirs."

"I don't..." *Ginny.* "Actually, I have a...friend..." Syd sucked in a quick breath. Referring to Ginny as a friend stung a little, but she didn't have time for involved explanations. "...who might be interested."

"Have them stop by the store. They aren't going to run a help wanted ad in the paper until next week."

The little boy strained against the hand that held him in place. "Grandma..."

"I better go before I have a meltdown on my hands."

Syd watched Kate maneuver her grandkids down the street

then looked back at the bookstore. She chewed her lip. It would be a perfect place for Ginny. They closed at eight every night, so the hours wouldn't interfere with her schoolwork. Maybe if her daughter had a job, she wouldn't feel so displaced. She'd mention it when she picked Ginny up from school. And that was another issue that needed some resolution. Transportation. Syd's work schedule and her daughter's school schedule didn't mesh. Ginny needed a car. The bank would make her a good deal on any one of a dozen repos. Maybe she could bring Ginny to the repo lot after school, and they could look at what was available. A job...a car... If Ginny had those things, maybe the transition would be easier. It wasn't really bribery. Syd chewed her lip as she walked. *Was it?*

Syd made it back to her office with twenty minutes of her lunch hour left. She spread a napkin on her desk, laid out her sandwich, and dumped out her chips. Her appetite fled as she stared at the food. She propped her elbow on the desk, rested her chin in her palm, and closed her eyes.

Father, I really need some direction here. I feel like You're telling me not to write Mason out of my life. I know Mason isn't Donny. But I've been so stupid where men are concerned. How can I know if it's really You urging me to give Mason a chance and not my own stupid, selfish desires? And if I can move beyond that, I don't know how to incorporate Mason into the new mix of me and Ginny. I was grasping at straws last night when I told Mason I had no time, but it's sort of true. I do need to spend my time with Ginny...

Syd sat up and rubbed at her temples. *Yeah, and making plans to get the girl a car and tell her about a job she might like frees up the evenings you told Mason were full.* She groaned as her head began to pound and leaned back in her chair. When had her life become a vicious circle?

Her cell phone rang from the depths of her purse. Syd grabbed the bag and fished among the receipts, breath mints, tissue packets, and aspirin bottles. Why couldn't she remember to use the side pouch intended for the phone? Her hand closed round the phone on the third ring. She pulled it free, noticed Ginny's name on the screen, and swiped the call open.

"Hi, sweetheart."

"Hey, um... You don't need to pick me up from school."

"Oh?"

"I've got a thing..."

"Something fun?"

Ginny's sigh echoed through the phone. "I signed up for the photography club. They have a meeting tonight, something about taking random photos for the yearbook. Kinsley Hubbard was in the office when I signed up. She says you know her mom, and she invited me to have dinner with her before the meeting."

Of course. Why hadn't she thought about introducing Ginny to Charley's daughter? The two girls would move in the same circles. They were both seniors this year. *I'm losing my mind.*

"That sounds great. How will you get home?"

"Kinsley will take me."

"How late will you be?"

Several seconds of silence greeted Syd's question. She lowered the phone and looked at the screen to make sure the call was still connected. Seconds ticked off on the tiny display.

"Ginny?"

"What's with the twenty questions? If it's a big deal, I'll just come home."

"I don't want you to *just come home*, sweetheart. I want you to have a good time with a new friend. But, we have work and school tomorrow. It's my job to know where you are, who you're with, and when to expect you home."

"I've been going out on my own for a couple of years now. You never cared before."

Syd rubbed at the spot of tension building between her brows. *I cared. Your grandparents have been in charge of those details.* It took a mighty effort to leave the words unsaid. "Let's do it this way. On school nights, I need you in the house by ten."

"That stinks!"

"Take it or leave it."

"Like I have a choice."

The phone went dead in Syd's hand, and she dropped it back into her bag. She'd call Charley later and make sure all of these plans were good on her friend's end.

Looks like dinner alone.

Yeah, well, what's new?

Her office phone startled her when it rang. Syd glanced at her uneaten lunch. How could it already be time for the calls to be routed back to this phone? The phone fell silent. Had she just ignored a call on her business phone? Really? She sat for a second and waited for it to ring again. When it didn't, she re-wrapped her sandwich. She'd have it for dinner tonight. She'd just nibble on the chips while she worked. Syd stood to take the sandwich to the small fridge in the corner. The edge of the napkin hung on something, and the chips scattered on the floor at her feet. She sank back into her chair, fighting back tears of frustration.

Syd scooted her chair back to her desk, cringing as the six little wheels ground chips into the carpet. She lowered her head into her hands and took some deep breaths.

She jumped when she felt a light touch on her shoulder.

"Syd?" Randy's voice was full of concern.

Great.

Syd raised her head, wiped a single tear from her cheek, and looked at her boss. "I don't suppose that if I said *amen* right now, you'd believe I was having a lunchtime talk with Jesus?"

Randy spared her a look, crossed to the office door, and looked outside. Obviously satisfied with what she saw, she closed the door and leaned against it. "Lying's a sin. If I let you get away with that, you really will need to say a prayer." She perched on the corner of Syd's desk. "You've been jumpy all morning. I let it go because…well, we all have those days. But I think there's more to it than a bad day. In all the years you've worked for me, I've never seen you in tears at your desk. Spill it."

Syd opened her mouth to deny it and snapped it shut when Randy held up a hand.

"And don't think I'll be satisfied with some mealy-mouthed platitude. My efforts at that didn't work with you when I was so upset over the situation with Eli and Astor a few years ago. You guys kept at me until you had the whole of the story. It was one of the best things that ever happened to me. I'm here, not as your boss, but as your friend, to return that favor." Randy opened the top drawer of Syd's desk and snatched a tissue from the box Syd kept there. She handed it to Syd. "It's after one. I can't lock this office down for long. Start talking."

Syd accepted the tissue and dabbed at her eyes. Thoughts flew through her mind. The story of her life with Donny and the mess he left behind was complicated and ugly. If she broke that silence, it wouldn't be only her life and reputation at risk but Sara's and Logan's as well. *Easy then, leave them out of it.*

"It's just everything with Ginny. This is a tough transition for her." Syd motioned to the phone. "She just called to say she's been invited to a friend's house. The good news is it's with Kinsley Hubbard. The bad news is that when I tried to impose a curfew, she got snotty and hung up. I've wanted her home for so long…prayed for it. She's been home three days, and I've barely seen her. Both of the girls begged me to let Ginny stay with Sara last night. I didn't mind. As much as I've missed my daughter, Sara missed her sister. It's just…I don't know. Right now, it's not feeling much like an answered prayer."

Randy tilted her head in thought. "It's tough on both of you. I'm no parenting expert, but I think love will win in the end. Not one of us is perfect, but you made every decision based on love for Ginny and what you thought was best for her."

Syd lowered her eyes and wished the truth were as sterling as Randy made it sound.

"She'll realize that eventually," Randy finished. "In the meantime, we're all praying for you both." She put a hand on Syd's shoulder. "Make me a promise?"

Syd looked up. "What's that?"

"Don't sit at your desk upset. You know you can talk to me." Randy's smile grew speculative. "And if you can't talk to me, there's a certain new guy in town who seems pretty willing to listen."

"Yeah, well..."

"Trouble there too?"

Syd bit her lip. Maybe it was time to squash that avenue as well. "I don't think there is a *there*. We talked last night, at least we tried. Things were pretty complicated after Anthony died. As much as I like Mason, I just don't feel like I should bring a new guy into the picture the same week Ginny comes home. That's not fair to her or him. I tried to make him understand that. I don't think I was very successful."

"What about what's fair to you?" Randy asked.

"Ginny has to come first." Syd congratulated herself on her answer. No one could argue that statement.

Randy studied Syd with slightly narrowed eyes. "You know, that's the most believable load of horse hockey I've ever heard."

"What?"

Randy stood to open the office door. "I'm not saying you're lying, just that I think there's a lot you're leaving out. I figure you'll get around to the whole truth eventually. For now, you stick with that story, and we'll keep praying. Since you don't have to rush home to be with Ginny tonight, and plans with Mason aren't an issue, I guess you can come over to Alex's with the rest of us and see what bee she has in her bonnet."

CHAPTER 9

*A*lex ushered Syd through the front door of her house later that evening. The tiled entry echoed with the voices of guests Syd could hear but couldn't see. Some of the voices were familiar, some not.

"Sorry I'm late," Syd said.

"We're still waiting on Mac." Alex hooked an arm around Syd's shoulders and turned her towards the dining room instead of the living room. "Everyone's in here."

"Careful with that one," one of the unfamiliar voices cautioned. "It's got enough sugar in it to take the top of your head off."

"Yes, but I believe those are little Snickers candy bars around the edge, and I'm an addict." Jesse's voice filtered up the hall, her laughter not quite hidden.

Syd stopped. "What's going on in there?"

Alex nudged her forward. "You have to see it to believe it, but I hope you're hungry."

Syd stepped into the dining room a half step ahead of Alex. Randy, Charley, and Jesse were there ahead of her. There was also a pretty Hispanic woman, a petite but older blonde, a woman with a short, shaggy brown hair cut, and a gorgeous brunette. The seven women were clustered at the far end of Alex's long dining room table huddled over four cheesecakes as if the desserts might sprout legs and take a hike.

Charley pointed at something brown topped with sprinkled nuts, a chocolate drizzle, and mounds of whipped cream. "What is that?" Wonder dripped from her voice like the chocolate dripping down the sides of the dessert.

"Nutella," the brunette supplied.

Charley's eyes went wide. "I just met you, but I think I love you."

"You guys are having way too much fun while I run back and forth to the door." Alex put her hands on her hips. "Somebody's gonna die if there isn't a piece of that lemon blueberry left for me." The women at the other end of the table looked up, some with guilty smiles. Alex pointed and introduced Syd, starting with the pretty Hispanic. "Syd, this is Lisa Sisko. She and her husband, Dave, pastor Valley View Church." She moved on to the blonde. "Callie Stillman."

Callie sent Syd a smile.

Alex came to the woman with the shaggy haircut and hesitated.

The woman licked chocolate from a finger and introduced herself. "Terri Evans."

Alex grinned. "Sorry, I'll get everyone sorted out by the end of the evening." She motioned to the remaining woman, the gorgeous brunette. "And this is Pam Lake. They're all a part of Valley View's women's group and responsible for the sinful assortment of desserts on the table. I made a pot of soup and some sandwiches, but they can't hold a candle to this."

"Life is short, eat dessert first." Terri forked up a bite of the Nutella cheesecake.

"Words to live by." Syd pointed to the offerings in turn. "Snickers, Nutella, and lemon." She stopped when she came to the final cake, the one Pam was slicing into pieces, the one covered with toasted coconut. "And this one?"

"German chocolate."

Syd sucked in a deep breath. "You guys are evil and should be burned at the stake." She picked up a plate and held it out to Pam. "Don't be stingy."

Laughter and the chime of the doorbell covered any response Pam might have made. Alex pointed at the assembled women. "I'll be right back. Don't forget what I said."

Alex was back in a flash with Mac in tow and another round of introductions began.

Mac held up a hand. "I already know everyone. Callie and Pam are regulars at the spa for manis and pedis. Terri and Lisa sneak in when their kids turn their backs long enough."

"Great." Alex spread her hand over the table. "We're starting our meeting with dessert. Pick your poison, and let's get started."

"Oh wow." Mac studied the choices. "Who can choose?" She rubbed her hands together. "I think I'll try all four."

Syd leaned back on her heels. "You really are sick."

Mac gave her a look.

"Sara mentioned she saw you at the clinic today. If the queen of fitness plans to indulge in four pieces of cheesecake, the diagnosis must be terminal."

Red crept up from Mac's collar and stained her face. "I...um... well..." She stuttered to a stop, and Syd took a step forward when she saw tears swim in her friend's eyes. "Whoa, Mac. What gives?"

Callie pulled out a chair and pushed Mac into it. "The diagnosis was nine months terminal, I'll bet."

The room froze at Callie's whispered words.

"More like seven," Mac whispered.

Syd would have bet money that she could've heard a pin drop onto the carpet.

Mac sucked in a breath and allowed her gaze to travel around the faces in the room. She stopped when she came to Callie. "How did you know?"

Callie patted Mac's hand. "Honey, I worked for an OB/GYN for more than twenty years. I know the signs. When we were talking the other day, you told me about your symptoms…pregnant was the first thing I thought.

At the word *pregnant*, the room came alive.

Jesse squealed and shoved everyone out of her way in her haste to get to Mac. She dropped to her knees next to the chair and took Mac's hands. "I'm going to be an aunt?"

Mac nodded.

"How's Dane?"

"Have you told Riley?"

"When are you due?"

"How are you?"

The questions were a blur to Syd, but Mac managed to sort them out. "The baby is due in April. Dane is walking around about three feet off the ground. We're driving to Tulsa this weekend to tell Riley that he's going to have a new sibling." She paused. "A baby." Her lip trembled. "My son is nineteen, and I'm having a baby." She swallowed before answering the last question. "How am I?" Mac swiped at her face with her sleeve. "Almost thirty-nine and pregnant."

Callie reached across the table, snagged a napkin, and pressed it into Mac's hand.

"Thanks." She mopped her face. "I've been crying all day. Dane actually thought I was unhappy. I just… I can't take it in. I'm having Dane's baby." Her hands went to her flat stomach. "Our baby." Her whispered words carried equal parts wonder and trepidation. "I'm excited…and I'm scared to death."

Jesse sat back on her heels. "Mom and Dad are going to have a cow."

Mac stared into Jesse's face. "Don't tell them, OK? Like I said, Dane and I need to tell Riley first. He's going to be… I don't know what he's going to be. I'm counting on shocked, I'm hoping for happy. Then your folks will be home for a few days next week. We want to tell them in person."

"I'd never ruin your surprise," Jesse promised. "But wow... Just wow."

Randy elbowed her way to the side of Mac's chair and handed her a plate with small pieces of the assorted desserts. "Let's give our little mother some room and get this show on the road. I've got a four-year-old who thinks she can't sleep if I'm not home."

Amid murmurs of consent, Alex brought a large pot of soup and a platter of sandwiches to the table, along with plates and bowls. "Y'all feel free to serve yourselves while we talk." The ten women found spots around the table with their cheesecake and their drinks. It was close, but Alex had the table extended to its full length.

Alex took the spot at the head of the table and waited while the others settled, smiling as, one by one, her guests looked her way expectantly.

"First, I want to thank everyone for coming out on a Tuesday night. I know we all have families and busy schedules." She sent Randy a smile. "I'll make this as brief as possible."

Alex hesitated, and Syd thought she looked a little lost, not quite sure where to start.

"God laid something on my heart a few months ago. Actually, six months ago." She looked at Jesse. "Before you married Garrett, you were so torn over the whole abuse and divorce thing. Your ex-husband was really messing with your head, and you had so many questions."

"Questions you guys had answers for," Jesse said, reaching for a sandwich. She filled a bowl with soup and held up the ladle. "Anyone else?" Five bowls were passed her way.

"Yeah," Alex said. "We had answers. We shared some scripture, talked it out, and helped you pray, but..."

Alex paused as if searching for the right words. She looked

around the table, her gaze lingering on her friends. "Child abuse, adoption stories, spousal abuse, even cult involvement."

Her eyes skated passed Syd.

You have a story too, daughter.

Syd looked away.

"We've all got a story that might help encourage others if we share them," Alex continued. "Ugly stories, but marvelous testimonies. We're so blessed because we have each other to share with and depend on. Not to have the right answer every single time, but…" She paused and looked at Lisa Sisko. "I don't think I'm explaining this very well. I saw something the other day… something about our past being someone else's road map."

The Valley View women looked at each other, and small smiles were exchanged. Pam leaned forward. "I think we can identify."

"Ecclesiastes says, 'A threefold cord is not easily broken,'" Terri provided.

"Exactly." Alex nodded. "Any one of us, as individuals, might have been crushed by the circumstances we faced. But having each other to lean on, knowing that we didn't face the hard times alone, gave us each the strength to persevere. That's a blessing we need to share."

"What do you have in mind?" Callie asked.

"A women's conference," Alex said. "A day of fellowship and sharing with the women in our community and further afield if they'll come. None of us faced our trials alone, and none of us is unique. Jesse, if you had questions regarding abuse and divorce, I know others do too and can be blessed by your story. Mac, God delivered you out of a cult. There probably aren't a lot of women in Garfield with that in their background, but I'll bet there are plenty of women living in bondage to something."

"You want us to share our stories?" Lisa asked.

"No pressure," Alex said. "Only if you feel the same tug in your spirit that I do."

"I'm in." Mac didn't hesitate. "If Riley can share with the youth group, I can share my experience with other women."

"Me too," Randy said. "If I'd had a better understanding of the scars child abuse can leave behind, maybe I wouldn't have been hit so hard when I had to face them. If I'd had the experience of others to learn from, maybe I wouldn't have been so afraid or ashamed to ask for help."

"Of course I'll share," Jesse chimed in.

"Me, too." Charley grinned. "If you think the story of an overly insecure adoptive mother is worth anything."

Alex gave her a thumbs up. "You guys are the best. Hunter's aunt has a friend who took in a young, pregnant rape victim a few years ago. Poor kid decided to keep her baby, and her father kicked her out. I've heard it's a wonderful story. I'd like to try and get Diana and Scottlyn to share it." Alex looked at Lisa. "Does this sound like something you'd be comfortable presenting to your women?"

"I think it's a wonderful idea." Lisa looked at the women who'd come with her. "Ladies?"

"How about learning to forgive yourself?" Callie asked.

"How about sincerely forgiving others?" Pam added.

"Or listening to God when you're sure He has it wrong." Terri smiled. "We'll have some more for you once we get with some of our friends and family who couldn't make it tonight."

Appetite gone, Syd listened to her friends, picked apart her piece of cheesecake, and had a silent but intense argument with God.

You have a story—

No way.

For My glory.

His glory and her shame. Not just hers. If it were just her, maybe…maybe she could do what He asked, but it wasn't her secret alone.

I have daughters who would be blessed by what I've done for you. Others who can avoid entrapment if they hear it from you.

All they'd know is what an idiot Syd was. That she'd put her daughters in harm's way.

They would know that I am mighty.

"No!"

"Syd?" Alex focused on her, head tilted to the side. "Did you say something?"

Syd snapped back to reality. Conversation around the table had died and everyone was looking at her. She cleared her throat and scooped up a bite of Alex's potato soup. "Nope, I'm good. It all sounds great." The words tumbled out of her mouth, fast and clipped...guilty. She focused on her bowl. *I can't do it, Father. I can't even share the truth with the people closest to me. How can You ask me to share with a bunch of strangers?*

Because I have given you much.

Oblivious to the internal battle Syd was waging, the conversation returned to Alex's plans. Talk of dates and locations, of how to get the word out.

"Once we decide on the details," Charley said, "maybe Melissa's husband could put his graphic design talents to use and put something special together for us."

"Good idea," Alex answered. "Could you ask him?"

Charley nodded. "I will, but for now, I need to get home. I left Kinsley with company and a pizza. They had a meeting to go to, but I'm sure I need to clean the kitchen, and I like to be home when she gets home."

Syd looked up, remembering that she hadn't said a word to Charley about their daughters. "Thanks for that by the way. I'm hoping Kinsley and Ginny can be good friends."

"I'm sure they will be. We are."

Syd watched Charley leave, knowing that she should do likewise but grateful for the small distraction from her troubled thoughts. It didn't last long.

Do this for me, daughter. I will give you the strength you need to be a blessing to others.

She shut the thought out of her head without a response. There was no way God, or anyone else, could talk her in to sharing the grief that Donny had put her and the girls through. She'd failed to protect her family once. She wouldn't fail again.

CHAPTER 10

hen the alarm sounded Wednesday morning, Syd sat up on the side of the bed feeling as if she hadn't slept thirty minutes the entire night. Between her indecision about Mason, Ginny's continued angst, and God's unrelenting prodding about Alex's project, there wasn't much room for rest. She lowered her head into her hands and rubbed her temples. It was just too much. She yawned. If she could move one thing off her plate, maybe she'd have the energy to deal with the others.

She dressed for her workout and knocked lightly on Ginny's door, pushing it open when she heard a murmured "What."

"Wake up, sleepyhead."

Ginny turned her back to Syd with a groan.

Armed with her cell phone, Syd crossed the carpet and sat on the side of the bed. She patted the rise of Ginny's hip. "Are you awake? I have something I want to show you."

"Yeah." The response was heavy with sleep.

Syd patted her daughter's hip again. "Slide up and look at me. I think you're going to like this."

Ginny flopped to her back and put an arm over her eyes. "What?"

Syd thumbed her phone to life and brought up the picture of the four-year-old royal blue Ford Focus she'd found in the bank's repo lot the afternoon before. She held it in the air over Ginny's face. "Take a look."

The arm came down and the eyes slitted open the barest fraction. "It's a car."

"Could be yours by the weekend."

Ginny jerked upright and reached for the phone.

"That got your attention."

Ginny scooted up against the headboard and looked at the small screen.

"I took a few shots of the interior as well."

The teen swiped through the other pictures before looking at her mother. "It's really nice."

"Yes it is," Syd agreed, "and I'm willing to pay half."

Ginny lowered the phone. "How much is half?"

Syd named a figure, and the excitement slipped from Ginny's face. "I have about a third of that in my savings." She dropped the phone onto the comforter. "Pipe dream." Rolling away, she slid back under the covers. "Close the door on your way out, will you?"

Syd gathered her patience around her and managed to keep her voice even. "Do you give up so easily? Seems like my half and your third would make a nice down payment. I work at the bank. They'd set us up with a reasonable payment. If you had a job—"

"I've been in town less than a week. I don't know of anyone looking to hire a student."

Syd grinned. "Oh, did I forget to mention that the local bookstore is looking for some after school help? Just light duty stuff. They haven't even advertised the position yet."

Ginny rolled over a little slower this time, eyes fully open, her attention focused on her mom. "The bookstore?"

"I'll admit that the distance between us hasn't made it easy to keep up with all your hobbies, but you still like books, don't you?"

Some of the ice melted out of Ginny's expression. "I love books. The smell, the feel, the weight in your hand. Letters making words, words making stories. A bookstore would be my dream job."

"I thought so. I'll give them a call—"

"No." A bit of frost returned to Ginny's eyes but it melted quickly. "Sorry, I didn't mean to snap. But I don't need you to pave my way. I'd like to do this on my own."

"That's fair," Syd said. "I'll pick you up after school and drop you off at the bookstore. You can walk to the bank once you're done, and we can take a look at the car. If that one doesn't suit you once you've seen it, there are others on the lot that might be a better fit." She stood, and the picture album that rested on the nightstand caught her attention. She picked it up and flipped through the pages. "Oh my." She sank back to the bed. "Sweetheart, these are wonderful. You've come a long way since you picked up your first camera. We should get some of these mounted and framed."

"Sara said the same thing."

"We should listen to her. These pale yellow walls would make a great backdrop for some of these." Syd stopped at a picture of a brilliantly colored hot air balloon floating in a sky ablaze with the pink and orange of a fiery sunset. "This is breathtaking. I'd love to have a Ginny Marlin original on my office wall."

"Really?"

"Really." She turned a few more pages and looked at Ginny. "You know, the bookstore sells some framed artwork. Maybe you could see if they'd be interested some of these."

Ginny's gaze grew speculative.

"With or without a job, we can make that a project if you like."

"Oh, I like."

"Good." She patted the book. "You might take this with you

and ask them about it. I have to leave for my workout. I'll be back in an hour to clean up and take you to school."

"Kinsley said she'd pick me up."

"Oh, good. I'm glad you two have hit it off." She reached for the doorknob and smiled a small self-satisfied smile when a "Thanks, Mom," reached her ears. She had no illusions about the war being over, but the pleasant start to her morning after such a rough night was a point in her favor. She'd take what she could get for now.

* * *

SYD MULLED the problem of Mason as she drove to the spa. He'd called again the night before just to say he was thinking about her. She hadn't taken the call, but she'd played the voicemail a dozen times. No matter how she twisted it, she didn't see a resolution. Mason was a terrific guy, thoughtful, considerate, and so easy to talk to. But Donny had deceived her with the very same traits eight years ago. Syd's family was still paying for her ignorance.

Trust me, daughter. I'll lead you down a straight path.

The words echoed in her heart but brought her no peace. Three years of being a Christian hadn't prepared her for this. "I do trust You, Father." She parked and sat with her head on the steering wheel. "It's me I can't trust."

She needed help. Syd looked up at the building. There was no way she could share the details of Donny's betrayal with her friends, but maybe there was another way.

Syd pushed the second story door open. Charley was there, warming up with some barbells. Alex sat on the floor, legs extended, stretching from one foot to another. Randy leaned against the wall, sipping from a cup of Ground Zero coffee. Mac and Jesse were missing.

"Morning. Where is everybody?" Syd asked.

"Not here yet," Charley said, her words in rhythm with her movements.

Randy shook her head at the impatient cop. "They aren't late, we're early."

Alex held onto the toes of her right foot and leaned into the stretch. "Have some patience," she grunted. She held the position for a few seconds then straightened. "Jesse's car wouldn't start. Mac was on her way out to pick her up when I came in. She promised an on-time start though. They still have five minutes."

Charley shelved the weights and took a swing at the exercise bag in the corner as she passed. "Didn't she just get that thing out of the shop?"

"Guess she didn't leave it long enough," Randy answered.

Syd looked at the clock and then at the door. Great, just when she had her courage screwed up to talk to her friends, half of them were missing. There must have been some telltale sign of frustration on her face.

"Problem?" the ever vigilant Alex asked.

"What? No...not really... I mean...I had something I needed to ask everyone. Actually, I have a...friend." Syd swallowed. Could she be any more transparent? "I have a friend who needs some direction. I thought you guys—"

The door swung open, and Mac and Jesse rushed into the room. Jesse looked pointedly at Charley. "Thirty seconds to spare."

Mac bent at the waist, her breathing heavy.

"You OK?" Randy asked.

Mac raised a hand. "I'm too old and pregnant to take those stairs at a run."

Randy closed the door. "Well, you have some time to catch your breath. Syd has a friend with a problem. She was just about to tell us about it."

Jesse snagged a couple bottles of water from the mini-fridge in the corner and handed one to the panting Mac before sitting on the mat. "What's up?"

Syd watched as the others found a place to sit. *That was way too easy.* Had they really bought into the whole *I have a friend* thing?

Alex patted the spot on the mat next to her. "So..." she prompted.

Syd sat and took a few seconds to give her story a thorough mental check before she spoke. She needed answers, but she didn't need to give away too much.

"I have a friend," Syd said. "She's got a couple of really hard choices to make, and she just can't seem to find any direction."

"Is she a Christian?" Alex asked.

"She's trying to be," Syd answered.

"And trying is all God asks of any of us." Alex laid a hand on Syd's knee. "I just meant has she prayed about the situation. Is she looking for, and listening for, God's will."

Syd nodded. "I know she reads her Bible, and she's been doing a lot of praying the last few days."

"That's perfect," Jesse said. "The Bible tells us not to be anxious about things, but to let our requests be made known."

Charley leaned forward. "I've always liked the verse in Proverbs that says if we acknowledge God, He'll make our paths straight."

"My favorite is in James." Randy tapped a finger against her lips. "I think it's in the first chapter, where he encourages us to ask for wisdom because He gives wisdom freely without reproach."

"Those are all great verses," Alex said. "Do we need to write them down for you...so you can give them to your friend?"

Syd chewed her lip. She needed so much more than Bible verses right now. The thought made her cringe. *Father, Your word is amazing, I just... I need something else.* "I know she's reading her Bible, and I'll share these verses with her, but the issue is sort of immediate. She's…umm…she's got a really messed up past." She pushed herself off the floor and went for her own bottle of water.

Syd made a half circle of the room before she continued, "A messed up past but maybe a chance for a happier future. She's made horrible mistakes. Mistakes she can't risk making a second time. I…she…" She took a deep gulp of the water, hoping the action would cover the near slip. "She feels like she's being pulled in two directions. Her experience is telling her one thing, God is *maybe* telling her something else, and the something else goes against everything she thinks she knows. It's a vicious circle."

Alex leaned back on her elbows. "Let me see if I've got this straight. Your friend feels like she's being told to do something impossible, and she's sure she's hearing it wrong."

Syd finished the circuit of the room and sat back down. "Pretty much."

Alex looked around the circle of friends. "Gideon."

"Yes," Mac said. "I love that story."

"Gideon?" Syd asked.

Alex smiled. "You haven't been a Christian for long, so I'm not surprised you don't know the story. Before there were kings in Israel, God chose a series of judges to rule over his people. Gideon was one of those judges, but before he was a judge, he was just a simple wheat farmer trying to make a living in a land besieged by enemies. God sent an angel to tell Gideon that he was chosen to save Israel. Gideon was pretty sure he'd heard wrong, and he wanted an unequivocal answer. So Gideon took the fleece of a lamb, put it on the ground, and told the Lord that if the guidance was really from Him, then to let the fleece be dry in the morning, but the ground all around it be wet."

Syd raised her eyebrows and waited for the punchline. "Well," she prompted.

"He got what he asked for," Alex said. "Dry fleece, wet ground."

"But"—Mac picked up the story—"Gideon still wasn't sure, so

he tried it again the next night. This time he told God to let the fleece be wet, the ground dry."

"He argued with God?" Syd asked. She started to say something else, but stopped when she realized she'd been doing the same thing. About Mason and about Alex's conference. She swallowed. "What happened?"

Mac giggled. "Wet fleece, dry ground."

"Really?" Syd asked.

"Really," Alex said. "God's not a magic eight ball or a genie in a lamp. Sometimes, in spite of prayer and everything else, we have to look hard for the answers we need. A fleece is a good tie breaker. But I don't recommend it for every situation. Some people misuse the process."

Syd tilted her head. "What do you mean?"

Alex thought for a second. "Like telling God, if it's Your will for me to forgive this person, let me win the lottery." She grinned. "That's extreme, but you see? Then, when the lottery thing never happens, they feel justified in not forgiving someone. The parameters of the fleece should never be about profit. And since we're commanded to forgive, there's no reason for a fleece."

"That makes sense."

"Good. If your friend is sincere and she's tried praying and searching the scripture with no clear cut direction, a fleece can't hurt."

"But she's got to be willing to accept the answer," Randy cautioned.

"I don't think that's a problem. She's pretty eager to have an answer."

"Anything else?" Mac asked.

Syd shook her head. "I think I... She'll know what she needs to do."

Mac scrambled to her feet, obviously enjoying a second wind. "Then it's time to sweat, ladies." She motioned to the speaker in the corner. "Charley, find us some music we can move to."

Ten minutes later, all six women were sweaty and breathless. Syd pondered Alex's suggestion while she kept time with the others. A fleece. Wet...dry. Dry...wet. She closed her eyes and envisioned her kitchen and the fresh dish cloth she'd placed over the divider between the sinks on her way out the back door this morning. Did she dare ask such a foolish thing of God? Why did the answer feel more complicated than the question?

Ask, daughter. I don't respect one child above another.

The words tangled up her feet, and Syd stumbled.

"Syd?" Mac asked.

"I'm fine, just clumsy this morning." She moved to the window at the back of the room to catch her breath and looked out over Garfield's main street. Mind made up, she closed her eyes and took a deep breath. *Father, I don't mean to be stubborn, but there's too much riding on this. I need an answer from You that I can't argue with. If You're telling me to trust Mason with my heart...with my family...then let that fresh rag be sopping wet when I get home.*

Fleece extended, Syd took her place back among her friends. There were other things she needed answers for, but lumping it all together seemed cumbersome. This process probably worked best with one question at a time. She stretched for her toes and couldn't wait for the session to be over.

CHAPTER 11

Syd jerked the car to a stop in her driveway, stabbed at the button that shut off the engine, and raced to her front door. She reached for the doorknob, twisted it, and bumped into it when it didn't move. She knocked on the door and called out for her daughter.

"Ginny." A frown materialized when Ginny didn't answer.

Kinsley picked her up.

Syd closed her eyes. Here she was, possibly standing on the brink of her own personal miracle, and she couldn't get in the house.

Keys.

Duh… She patted the pockets of her shorts, came up empty, and reached for her purse, turning in a half circle before she realized it wasn't hanging from her shoulder. She sent a self-conscience look up and down the street. Her neighbors would think she'd lost her mind. Returning to the car at a more leisurely pace she reached in and retrieved her bag. The keys were right in the pocket they always occupied.

This time when she reached the front door, she paused. *Father, I don't even know what I'm expecting. I just want to know Your will for me and my family. I promise that I'll do my best, whatever Your answer is.*

When the door swung open, Syd went straight to the kitchen. From the doorway she could see the dish cloth right where she'd left it. *Does it look darker than it should?* Her feet refused her command to move forward. She forced one foot in front of the other until she stood at the sink. One finger reached out to touch the brown terry cloth. Syd jumped when it came back wet. She yanked her hands behind her back.

Oh wow...oh wow...

Bending for a closer examination, she could see that the cloth was soaked with water, leaving small rivulets running down the stainless steel of the sink.

Ginny must have used it.

The thought gave Syd pause. She wanted to reject the negative voice inside her head, but it was possible. And it was possible she was acting like a doubting Thomas. That story she knew.

But she'd asked for an irrefutable answer. The cloth she'd left dry on the sink was wet, but other explanations, explanations that weren't heavenly, existed. She couldn't very well call Ginny during class to ask if she'd used the fresh dishcloth. Tears gathered in Syd's eyes. She'd so hoped...

She straightened. There was more to Alex's story than a single attempt. Maybe it took the whole process to get the whole answer.

OK.

Syd closed her eyes. "Father, I promised to do my best with the answer You gave me, but I don't think we're there yet. I'm going to get ready for work. I'm the only person in the house, so Your answer will be plain. If Mason is supposed to be a part of my life, let this thing be completely dry when I'm ready to walk out the door."

In the back of the house, Syd showered, did her hair, and applied her makeup for the day. All the while, she fought the urge to return to the kitchen and instead forced herself into a patience she didn't really feel. *The process might not work if I rush it.*

She picked out a turquoise and brown skirt, added a matching blouse, and slipped on her new brown pumps. She took her time over her jewelry selection, spritzed on her favorite perfume, and grabbed her purse. She was ready. Was God? She bit her lip and looked at the clock. Almost an hour had passed since she got home. A shudder of anticipation ran across her shoulders.

What if it was dry?

Syd swallowed. Dry meant extending trust in a situation where she'd suffered nothing but heartbreak. It meant exploring a relationship with Mason.

But it might still be wet.

Wet meant no Mason in her future, but it meant living life in the comfort zone she'd established for herself.

Risk or denial? Which did she want? Was it even up to her?

Syd's steps were hesitant as she moved down the hall. She peeked around the corner. The rag was right where it had been an hour ago. She squinted across the room, anxious to see if anything was different. *You're gonna have to pick it up.*

Syd took a deep breath and crossed the room in six long strides. She closed her hand over the rag and froze. Dry wasn't even a word she could use. It was as if the cloth had been baked in the dessert sun and hadn't seen a drop of water in a year. It was brittle dry.

She released it, backed up against the opposite counter, and stared. "Oh my dear Lord." She put a trembling hand over her mouth. What was she supposed to do now?

Trust Me, daughter. I have good plans for you.

Syd's mouth went dryer than the cloth. She blew out a deep breath. OK, she'd made a promise. The next move was hers.

Except she had no idea what that might be.

Her phone rang, and she reached for it blindly, pulled it from the pocket of her bag, and swiped the connection open with her eyes still on the rag that dared dictate her future.

"Hello."

"Syd, thank goodness."

Instead of the impatience she deserved after two days of silence, Mason's voice was warm. The phone almost slipped from Syd's hand as her eyes cut to the ceiling.

"Hi." The word squeaked past her lips, and Syd cringed. She cleared her throat and tried again. "Good morning, Mason." She turned her back on the sink. "How's everything?"

"Better now that I'm hearing your voice. I've been worried about you. You rushed out of here Monday night like a raccoon with a hound on its tail."

"Sorry. I just…" She just what? She still couldn't explain the issues that had driven her out of his house, and she sure couldn't tell him about… She glanced over her shoulder. The *fleece* was still there, mocking her or encouraging her, she couldn't be sure. "I'm sorry about the way I acted the other night. Can you forgive me?"

"Of course. I just wanted to know you're OK."

"I'm fine. I…uh…" Syd gulped air into her lungs and threw herself off the emotional cliff she was standing on. Hopefully God would give her wings before she smacked the ground in a spread-eagle sprawl. "I was going to call you…later. I wondered if you had plans for Saturday night."

There was the tiniest pause before Mason said, "As it happens, I don't."

"I'd like to fix dinner for you. I'd like for you to meet my daughters and my grandson." The second the invitation was out of Syd's mouth, something dark and heavy lifted from her shoulders. She actually felt her back straighten. The release sent tears coursing down her face. One word rang in her heart.

Freedom.

Did this single act of trust finally free her from the hurt of Donny's betrayal?

"Syd?"

She sniffed, reached behind her, grabbed the rag, and dabbed at her face. "I'm here."

"I said I'd enjoy that very much."

Syd smiled through her tears. "OK, it's a date. I'll call you Saturday morning with details."

"May I call you tonight? I miss our chats."

"Absolutely," Syd answered. "I need to let you go. I'm going to be late." She swiped the call closed, replaced the phone, and looked at the rag in her hands, wet now with the tears of her release. She took it back to her room. She wasn't sure what she should do with it, but she planned to keep it in a special place. She...

Her phone rang a second time. Sara this time.

"Hel—"

"Mom, I need you to come. They want Logan at the hospital, right now. Children's Hospital."

"What? Did they—?"

"I don't know anything." Panic dripped from her daughter's words. "Dr. Joe just called and told me to bring him to the ER, now."

"Mommy."

Syd heard her grandson's plaintive cry through the connection.

"Mom, I've got to go. Can you come?"

"Yes," Syd answered. "I'll be there in thirty minutes."

"Please hurry."

The phone went dead in Syd's hands.

* * *

Ninety minutes later Syd pulled up under the awning of the emergency room entrance at Children's Hospital in Oklahoma City. "Hang on, I'll get the door." She slipped the gear shift into park, ran around to the passenger side, and opened the door. She took Logan, who was bundled in a blanket, from Sara and held him close while her daughter climbed out of the car. She kissed his forehead and passed the boy back to his mother. "I'll be right behind you."

Fear tugged at Syd's heart as she watched two of the people she loved most in the world walk away from her. Her teeth worried her lower lip. *What's waiting on the other side of that door?* The question was pointless, and she shoved it aside, swiping anxious tears from her face at the same time. Worry wouldn't provide any answers. She got back behind the wheel and saw a car backing out of a space fifty feet from the door.

With a quick look in her mirrors and the sure knowledge that God provided in every situation, Syd gave the car some gas, coasted into the spot, and hurried back through the sliding glass doors of the busy ER. Scents and noise greeted her. Antiseptic, the sharp sting of alcohol, an underlying bitterness as if someone might have recently vomited on the tile floor. Over the low murmur of waiting patients, a baby cried, and there was the soft sound of hurried footsteps from the staff.

A door in a side wall swung open, and Sara, still holding Logan, was about to step through. "Wait, I'm here." They paused, and Syd slipped through the automatic door before it had a chance to shut her out.

The nurse frowned. "I'm afraid you need to wait—"

"This is my mom," Sara said. "I need her with me."

"Yes, of course. Follow me." The nurse led them to a small treatment room and indicated the bed. "Why don't you lay him down there? I need to take his vitals and get some information."

"I need to know what's going on." Sara put Logan down on the bed and smoothed his hair out of his face. "Why did Dr. Joe insist that we bring Logan straight to you?"

The nurse bent over Logan and ran a thermometer across his forehead before fastening a blood pressure cuff around the child's skinny upper arm. "How you doing, buddy?"

"I don't feel so good."

She made some notes on a tablet before patting Logan's arm. "I know, but we're going to try and fix that for you." She glanced up and addressed Sara. "The doctor is on his way. I know it's hard to wait, but it's best if you get your answers from him. Five minutes, OK?"

Sara folded her arms around herself and nodded before leaning her head on Syd's shoulder. Syd slipped an arm around her daughter's waist, torn between worry for her child and worry for her grandson. Everything about the situation whispered of trouble. She rubbed Sara's back, doing her best to lend some comfort and breathed a prayer. "Father, send us Your presence in this place."

Logan sat straight up. "Mommy, I'm gonna be sick."

The nurse grabbed a small basin, held it under Logan's chin with one hand and wrapped the other arm around the child's shoulders. There wasn't much left in his stomach, but the uncontrollable heaving brought fresh tears to Syd's eyes.

When the spasm released Logan, his shirt, the sheet and the nurse's scrubs were dotted with vomit.

Logan finally looked up, his own eyes bright with moisture. "I'm sorry."

"It's OK," the nurse whispered. "All that's important is that you feel better. Do you feel better?"

"A little."

"Good." She tossed the basin and its contents into a can lined with a red bio hazard bag. Next, she stepped to the door and spoke to someone on the other side before coming back to the bed and pulling away the soiled sheet. "Let's get rid of this and get you into something clean. That'll make you feel even better, won't it?"

"Yeah, but"—Logan pointed at the spots on the nurse's sunflower printed scrubs and looked at her with wide, pitiful eyes—"I got my puke on you."

A light knock sounded at the door before it swung open to admit a second nurse carrying fresh sheets and a small hospital gown printed with images of super heroes.

"It's OK, buddy. I know you didn't mean to, and I have plenty of extras. Let's get you cleaned up, and then I'll take care of me." She handed the gown to Sara. "If you'll help him change, I'll take care of the bed."

Sara lifted Logan from the bed and stood him on the floor. "Hands up."

Logan raised his arms high, and Sara stripped the shirt off.

Syd gasped and tried to stifle the sound with a hand over her mouth. Logan's torso was a network of ugly purple bruises.

Sara glanced her way, her lips in a grim line. She pulled Logan close and tied the gown behind his back, mouthing "It's awful," before she allowed the boy to take a step back. "All done," she said and Syd knew the smile on Sara's face was forced for Logan's sake.

"Me too," the nurse said. She patted the mattress. "Climb back up here for me."

Logan did as instructed while the nurse asked him some questions.

"I see Superman, the Hulk, and Spider-man on that gown. Who's your favorite?"

"Captain America."

"Really?" She took a step back and studied her patient. "Why?"

"Because he's really fast and strong. His shield is sort of like a big Frisbee. I'm practicing so I can throw it just like him." He tilted his head and gave her a gapped-tooth smile. "Who do you like?"

Before she could answer, a second knock sounded at the door and two men crowded into the small room. One was Dr. Joe. The other was an older man with thinning hair and a pleasant smile. He carried a purple Popsicle.

Logan perked up. "Hey Dr. Joe. *Buenos días.*"

Dr. Joe's brilliant white smile lit his dark face. "*Buenos días* to you, young man. He stepped to the side of the bed and ruffled the boy's hair. You'll have to put a sucker on my account. My pockets are *vacía.*"

Logan frowned over the new word. He whispered it aloud, rolling it around on his tongue.

"*Vacía.*" Dr. Joe repeated the word slowly and patted the flat pockets of the lab coat he wore. "*Vacía* means empty."

"That was a hard one."

"But you tried. Do you like grape Popsicles?"

Logan tilted his head so that he could look at the stranger. "*Mucho.*"

"You are an incorrigible imp." He nodded to the stranger, who placed the treat into Logan's waiting hands. "Two suckers on account and one grape Popsicle."

"*Gracias.*"

"Enough." Dr. Joe laughed. "We've got to get out of here before this boy breaks me." He looked at the nurse. "You two keep each other company for a few minutes. We need to speak to Logan's mom and grandma."

Despite the smiles and teasing between doctor and patient, the atmosphere in the room had thickened with each word. Something in the tone of his voice, some stiffness in his bearing, told her Logan's doctor did not have any good news to share.

* * *

SARA WAITED for the door to close behind them before she crossed her arms and planted her feet. "I need to know what's going on."

The two men looked at each other, and something unspoken

passed between them. Dr. Joe nodded and motioned the other man forward. "This is Dr. Price. He's the leading pediatric oncologist in the state."

Oncologist. The word hit Sara with the force of a punch. She reached blindly for her mother's hand, found it, and clung for dear life. She faced Dr. Joe, ignoring the other man as if not acknowledging him would make him go away. "Why does my son need an oncologist?"

Dr. Price was not so easily dismissed. "Ms. Marlin, if you'll follow me, there's a small meeting room at the end of the hall. We can talk there."

"I'm not budging until someone answers my question."

"Sweetheart, maybe…" Her mother's voice was a strangled whisper. Sara ignored it and continued to stare at the doctors.

Dr. Price's sigh was heavy with resignation. "Your son's platelet count is dangerously low. We need to run some further tests."

Sara studied the doctors. "Tests for what?"

"Leukemia."

The word stole Sara's breath. Her ears rang and her vision darkened around the edges. "Leu…" Her knees buckled, and she would have crumpled to the floor if Dr. Joe hadn't taken a swift step to her side and put a steadying arm around her waist.

"Sara?"

She heard her mother's voice from far away and fought to focus on it.

"Sara."

This time the word was a little firmer, but the sound of tears in her mother's voice drove the panic of the moment deeper. Sara gasped for breath. Someone pressed a plastic cup into her hand.

"Drink that and take some deep breaths." Dr. Joe's voice held more command than she'd ever heard.

Cool hands wrapped around the sides of her face. Her mother's tearful expression swam into focus. "Sara, look at me."

Sara blinked and tried to focus, but her mother's face kept fading in and out. Someone took the cup from her hands and brought it to her mouth.

"Take a small drink," Mom said.

She did and nearly choked as she swallowed, but the cold water helped.

Her mother spoke again. "Logan needs his mother now more than ever." A comforting arm wrapped around her and she heard a whispered prayer in her ear. "Jesus, give her strength."

This can't be happening, not to my baby.

Sara swallowed again and pulled away slightly as the world solidified. She looked at her mom and saw her own fears mirrored in her mom's eyes. Her gaze went to the doctors. There was no reassurance in their grim faces. Sara found her mother's hand a second time as she nodded down the hall. "Lead the way."

CHAPTER 12

*S*yd kept Sara's hand firmly in her own as they followed the doctors to the empty room. Her mind whirled. *Leukemia.* She couldn't grasp it. Not Logan. Not the happy, rambunctious little boy who never slowed down. Except he had.

God, please... Syd swallowed, and the request died an ugly death in her heart. She couldn't even pray. There were no words for this situation.

A glance at Sara told her that her daughter was in no better place. Her face was a colorless palette marked only by the shine of streaming tears. She shuffled along beside Syd like a cast member from a zombie movie, eyes staring straight ahead, body stiff. Her grip on Syd's hand was crushing in its intensity.

Sara must have felt Syd's gaze on her. She glanced in her mother's direction, her normally vibrant blue eyes flat and lifeless. She opened her mouth to speak, but the quivering of her chin stopped her.

Syd squeezed her hand, doing her best to transfer part of her own failing strength to her daughter.

The doctors ushered them into a small room. A single table and half a dozen chairs filled the space. The walls were lined with cabinets and hung with colorful inspirational posters obviously geared toward children. Syd took the seat offered to her and stared at the poster on the opposite wall. It was blue, and the words were written in a childish scrawl with different colored crayons. *You never know how strong you are until strong is the only choice you have.* She had just a moment to wonder if that was directed at the parent or the child before Dr. Joe cleared his throat and took Sara's free hand in his. A chain of hope and despair.

"Sara, Mrs. Patterson, I know this has blindsided you, and I know you have lots of questions. Perhaps if you allow Dr. Price to explain, you'll have a better grip on those questions."

Syd nodded when Sara turned her way, a scared child looking for direction in a world suddenly gone haywire. "I think that's good advice," Syd whispered. Her words were hoarse. She needed information as badly as her daughter.

Dr. Price rested his arms on the table and laced his fingers together. "Dr. Joe called me when he received the results of Logan's blood work for a couple of reasons. When we consider the test results and the symptoms that Logan's had…" He sighed. "I want you to listen carefully to what I'm about to say. Leukemia is a scary word. The diagnosis is serious, but I want you to understand that great strides have been made in treating this disease."

"Mono." Sara looked at Dr. Joe. "You said you thought it was mono."

"That was my initial thought, but the tests don't bear that out. We need to test Logan for acute lymphoblastic leukemia, a cancer of the blood."

Sara groaned and bowed her head. Syd scooted her chair closer and held her daughter.

The doctor continued, "Acute lymphoblastic leukemia, commonly called ALL, is the most common form of childhood leukemia. With aggressive treatment, remission can be achieved in about ninety-eight percent of patients. Ninety percent of those can be completely cured."

"Did you hear that?" Dr. Joe asked.

Syd and Sara both turned to him.

"If Logan has ALL, the odds of recovery are very high."

"Very high," Dr. Price agreed, "but we need to get a definitive diagnosis. If ALL is confirmed, we need to start him on chemotherapy immediately."

Syd cocked her head. "You aren't sure?" she asked, grasping at the thin thread of hope.

The doctors exchanged a glance. "Eighty percent sure," Dr. Joe said. "We need to do a bone marrow test to be one hundred percent."

"Today?" Sara's single word was a stilted squeak directed to Dr. Joe. She cleared her throat. "You want to do that today?"

"The sooner the better," he answered.

Sara straightened, and Syd was relieved to see some color and fight coming back into her daughter's face. "What does this test consist of?"

Dr. Joe motioned to Dr. Price. The older man stood, crossed to a bank of cabinets, and returned with a handful of illustrated diagrams. He handed them to Dr. Joe, who arranged them in front of Sara.

Dr. Price pointed to the first sheet. "We need to collect a sample of Logan's bone marrow. Bone marrow is the place where blood cells are made. The best location for sample collection is inside the hip bone."

Sara sucked in a breath and pointed to one of the pictures, which showed a diagram of a large needle buried deep inside the bone of a patient. She looked at her mother. Anxiety had etched deep lines in her face. "Mom…"

Dr. Price seemed to read her mind. "We'll put Logan to sleep for the procedure. He won't feel any pain."

"It's safe?" Syd asked.

"No surgical procedure is risk free. The site could bleed more than expected. If Logan's immune system has been compromised, he could develop an infection. These dangers are low when weighed against delaying an accurate diagnosis."

Sara swiped at her eyes with her sleeve. "If you do this today, how long will it take? You said there was a chance that Logan didn't have this...thing. Will we have results today?"

Dr. Joe answered her questions. "The procedure takes about thirty minutes. Most of that time is needed to prepare the patient and to care for him post anesthesia. A priority will be put on the sample. We should have the results by the end of the day, no later than first thing in the morning." He leaned in and looked from Sara to Syd and back. "Sara, I know you're holding onto the slim chance that we're wrong. That's not a bad thing, but if you can hold onto the twenty percent and brace yourself for the eighty percent, that's what you need to do."

Sara's nod was a single quick jerk of her head. "What do I tell my son?"

"Just the basics for now." Dr. Price answered. "This is just another test to try and find out what's making him sick and fix it. If we need to tell him more later, we have people here who can help you explain."

"OK." Sara stood and held out a hand to Syd. "I want to get back to Logan."

"One more thing." Dr. Joe stopped her retreat with an upraised hand. "I know you two are Christians. Dr. Price and I are as well. It is our habit, whenever we can, to ask God to partner with us in the patient's care." His brilliant smile flashed. "Would you like to join us in that prayer?"

Sara crumpled back into her chair, tears flowing like twin rivers down her face.

Syd stepped behind her and wrapped her arms around her daughter's heaving shoulders. She fought her own tears as she said, "We'd both appreciate that."

The doctors moved so that one stood on either side of the huddled women. Syd closed her eyes as they reached out to lay a hand on each shoulder. Dr. Joe's voice rumbled through the room.

"Jesus, thank You for being in this place in our time of distress. Thank You because You have given us great resources. You control our ability. You control the results. This is key, that we always recognize that You are in control of this situation and the days that lie ahead."

Dr. Price picked up the prayer. "We're asking You to guide us through every step of this process. Let there be comfort and relief for Logan. Help his family find Your peace. Give all the staff involved in Logan's care compassion and wisdom at all times."

Dr. Joe took over. "Jesus, we ask these things in Your marvelous name. Amen."

Syd opened her eyes. Still seated, Sara wept. The eyes of both doctors were alight with moisture, their expressions full of compassion and resolve.

"Thank you," Syd whispered.

Something rattled in Dr. Price's pocket. He took out a phone, glanced at the screen, and stepped to the door. "I need to take this."

Once he left, Dr. Joe looked at the women. "I'll be on Logan's team, but Dr. Price will be the team captain. Let's get Logan admitted."

* * *

THE ROOM ASSIGNED to Logan seemed too big for the little patient drowsing in the bed. The wall over the bed was crowded with monitors and machinery that had functions Syd could only guess at. The thought of seeing Logan attached to them forced her to look away. *Not my sweet baby. Please, God, don't punish him for my guilt.*

The unbidden thought drew a gasp, and Syd raised a hand to cover the sound. Still, it echoed in the room.

"Mom?"

Syd turned to find Sara's gaze on her. Sara was seated in a chair pulled next to Logan's bed. She had his small hand clutched in hers, and her eyes were red from weeping over her sleeping child. "Did you say something?"

"Just thinking. You doing OK?"

Sara shrugged. "I wish they'd hurry already." She looked at the closed door and back at her son. Syd saw the tremor as Sara stroked his hair. "A little bit of me died when they said leukemia." Her voice broke, and Syd saw her struggle for composure. "I didn't think things could get worse. I was wrong. The waiting is going to kill me. Even if the knowing is bad, I need to know." She closed her eyes and shifted to rest her head on Logan's hand.

Syd went back to her pacing, her praying, and her guilt. Guilt was an old enemy. Guilt over her own gullibility. Guilt over failing to protect her family. There was even a lingering amount of guilt, small but ever present, that reminded her that if she'd been the wife Donny needed, he wouldn't have...probably wouldn't have... She erected a road block right there, complete with flashing yellow lights, warning her that this path led to madness. Madness she'd worked hard to eradicate from her life.

But this variation was new.

Don't punish Logan.

The words appalled her, and she sent a plea heavenward. *Father, You wouldn't, would You? Donny is a monster. Sara could have said no, but she was just a child, coerced by threats. I should have seen and didn't. But Logan? He's the one true innocent involved here.*

A brisk knock sounded at the door an instant before it was pushed open to admit Dr. Price.

"How's our patient?"

Sara sat up. "Sleeping."

"What we gave him for nausea will do that. Once we get him to the back, we'll give him a little something extra to keep him calm."

"You said he'd be asleep." Sara's voice rose with panic.

"Completely," Dr. Price assured her. "But we won't administer the full anesthesia until it's time for the actual procedure."

Two nurses followed the doctor into the room. They recorded Logan's vital signs and then looked at Dr. Price. He gave them a quick nod, and they raised the side rails of the bed and released the wheels. Sara didn't move from her place by the bed, didn't release Logan's hand.

The doctor joined her. "He's in good hands, Sara. You may not trust mine yet, but you can trust God's."

Sara's eyes filled as she leaned down to brush Logan's cheek with a kiss.

Syd did the same from the other side.

"We'll have him back to you in no time," Dr. Price said.

One of the nurses added, "While you wait, you've got some visitors gathered down in the waiting room. I'm sure they'd appreciate an update."

Syd stepped away from the bed and watched as they maneuvered it out of the room. She took Sara's hand and pulled her to the door. "Thirty minutes. He'll be back before you know it."

Syd and Sara trudged to a waiting room that tried and failed at homey. Chairs and sofas covered in bright primary colored vinyl cushions lined the space. It could have been a cheerful room in any other setting but there was no escaping the antiseptic smell that filtered in from the hall. But, they had the room to themselves. Syd, Sara, and a group of ever faithful friends.

Thirty minutes stretched into ninety. Nurses had come to the waiting area twice to assure them that the delay was caused by an unexpected complication with the patient proceeding Logan, not with Logan himself. The news was both comforting and not.

While they waited for word, Syd divided her time between

her daughter and her friends. Her earlier panicked call to Randy detailing what they'd been told and asking for prayer had brought them all running, ready to offer what support they could.

Randy and Alex had arrived first, already there when Syd and Sara arrived. Jesse and Mac came next. It was inching past four-thirty, and they'd brought bags of burgers and take out drinks. Syd encouraged Sara to eat, even though the thought of food settled on Syd's stomach like a lead weight.

"I'm not hungry," Sara told her. But she grabbed a soda and sipped on it.

Charley came with Ginny in tow. The younger girl's eyes were red-rimmed, and Syd wrapped her in a tight hug.

"Leukemia, Mom?"

Syd fought back her own emotion. "It's a possibility, but we're praying that they're wrong." She broke the embrace, slipped an arm around Ginny, and led her to the couch where Sara sat. "Sit with your sister. Jesse and Mac brought burgers for everyone if you're hungry."

"I'm not," Ginny answered.

"That's what your sister said. But maybe you two could share one."

Sara said, "Mom—"

"I could do that," Ginny put an arm around Sara's shoulders. "Come on, sis, four or five bites. It'll do you good."

Syd smiled her gratitude at her younger daughter and mouthed a quick *thank you* as Ginny settled onto the cushions, reached for the sack of burgers, and gave Sara her full attention. Ginny might resent her mother, but the girls were close despite the eight years of separation. Ginny would do what she could to keep Sara from dwelling on the worst. Syd closed her eyes as a fresh wave of fear and guilt washed over her. She stepped out into the hall. Randy started to follow, but a quick motion of Syd's hand kept her friend in place.

Syd leaned on the wall just outside the door and closed her eyes. *Please, Father, not leukemia. Please don't punish my children any further for my mistakes. I thought... I thought when I was obedient to You earlier that things would smooth out. I know You have a plan, not just for Mason and me but for my daughter and her child—*

"Syd?"

Her eyes snapped open. Mason stood close, and she allowed him to take her hands in his. His smile made her weak in the knees, and even in these dire circumstances his touch came with a bolt of electricity straight to her heart.

He squeezed her hand. "How you holding up?"

"I've had better days. Thanks for coming."

"Of course. Is there anything I can do?"

In direct opposition to the weak knees and shocked heart, the compassion etched on his face comforted her. He'd come when she needed him. "Pray. Sara is a basket case and"—she had to stop and swallow—"I'm not much better."

"Of course," Mason answered. "Anything else?"

"I'd kill for a cup of decent coffee."

"Let me see what I can do."

Once he'd gone, Syd stepped back into the waiting room. Sara and Ginny huddled together on a sofa, whispering over the burger that was slowly but surely disappearing. On the other side of the room, the best friends Syd had ever had talked quietly. Their physical presence was a wall of support. They didn't press for details, but Syd knew they were praying, knew they'd be there to offer whatever she needed, whenever she needed it. She went to them and allowed them to enfold her while the wait stretched into its second hour.

CHAPTER 13

*S*ara leaned her head against the back of the sofa. She didn't know how much longer she could sit here without losing her mind. Her baby, her reason for living, was somewhere down the hall undergoing a test for cancer. The thought sent terror slithering down her spine.

Cancer.

Leukemia.

Illness.

Death.

The words joined hands, formed a circle, and did a little mocking dance around her heart.

God?

I'm here, daughter. Trust me. I take care of the sparrows, and your son is much more valuable than they.

Tears slid down the side of her face. *I do trust You.* Breath hitched in and out of her lungs. *Father, this day has been a week long. I need word, I need—*

"Ms. Marlin?"

Sara lunged to her feet. A nurse stood in the doorway. Sara

hurried across the room. Her mom met her there and put an arm around her shoulders. "I'm Ms. Marlin. Is Logan OK?"

"He's tucked up, safe and sound in his room. He's awake and a little uncomfortable, nothing that a mild painkiller won't fix. We're gonna take care of that right away. He's asking for you."

Sara let out a breath and squeezed her mom's hand. "Thank you. When can we see Dr. Price?"

"He would have come straight here, but he was detained by an emergency. Go on along to Logan's room. The doctor will be in to visit with you shortly."

* * *

SARA ALMOST RAN to Logan's bedside. She grabbed his hand. "Baby, are you OK?"

"Hurts."

The single word, delivered in such a mournful whisper, shattered Sara's already broken heart. "Oh, baby. Mommy's here. It'll be OK."

Logan didn't respond, but his little face was a tense mask. Sara looked up as her mother moved to the other side of the bed and brushed the hair from Logan's forehead. "Where is that nurse?" she whispered.

As if summoned by her words, the door opened and admitted the nurse and Dr. Price. The nurse had a small plastic pouch in one hand and a cup of something clear in the other. She set the cup on the bedside table, hung the bag on the IV pole, and attached the line to the IV drip already flowing into Logan's arm.

"Just a little intravenous acetaminophen," she told Sara. "An injection would be insult to injury at this point, and the oral suspension might upset his stomach. This will work faster, and he won't feel a thing besides better."

She finished and patted Logan's arm. "How you doing, sport? Are you hungry?"

Logan shook his head without opening his eyes.

"That's a shame. I think the kitchen has a chocolate milkshake with your name on it."

Logan's eyes came open.

"Thought that might get your attention." The nurse removed a couple of packages of crackers from her pocket. "I'll make a deal with you. There are four crackers here. You eat these and drink the Sprite in this cup. We'll let that rest in your tummy for thirty minutes. If the crackers don't make you sick, you get the milkshake. Deal?"

"Deal." The word held a little bit more of the spunkiness Sara expected from her son. It bolstered her spirits.

"Good," the nurse said. "I'll raise your bed a bit and get you started while your mom talks to Dr. Price."

Logan cut his eyes to Sara, and his voice quivered. "Don't leave."

"I'm only going as far as the door, I promise." Logan didn't answer, but Sara felt his eyes on her as she and her mother joined the doctor.

Dr. Price hung his hands in the oversized pockets of the long, white lab coat. "Your son's a real trooper, and the procedure went fine. As you can see, he's a little uncomfortable, but that's to be expected and easily controlled."

"And the test results?" Sara asked.

The doctor expelled a long breath. "I know I told you that we'd probably have the results today, but we weren't expecting the two-hour delay in getting the procedure done. We're going to do everything we can to get the results this evening but it will likely be morning before the pathologist gets to Logan's sample. I'm sorry."

Sara stared at him. "Tomorrow?" *God, help me.* How would she make it through the night with this hanging over her head? She'd spent almost six hours working up her courage. Trying to find the backbone to support her son when they had to tell him...what?

"I know the waiting is hard, I wish I could give you better news." He motioned to the room. "You can stay with him of course. And once he goes to sleep, I have a job for you."

Sara raised a brow.

"We're going to need a list of possible bone marrow donors."

"You don't even have the results yet."

"Finding a donor is often a lengthy process. We need to start testing as soon as we can in case we have need of one down the road. We'll start with immediate family. You, his father..."

The doctor rattled on about the people she could add to her donor list. Sara didn't hear anything after the word *father*. Cold dread pooled in her stomach. She looked at her mother and saw a similar emotion. No way was she bringing Logan's father into this.

No. Way.

* * *

MASON SIPPED his cooling coffee and tried to control his impatience. By the time he'd come back with the two cups of coffee, Syd and her daughter had been called away. He looked around the waiting room, a lonely man in a sea of women. His daughter-in-law, Jesse, sat in the corner with her huddle of friends. They spoke in low voices, casting occasional glances at the door, obviously as anxious for news as he was. The only other person in the room was a young woman who sat by herself, turning pages in a large book. He'd not been introduced but guessed that this was Syd's newly arrived daughter, Ginny. Odd that she wasn't with the rest of the family.

The women had, one by one, made an attempt to pull Mason into their circle. He'd stood among them for a few minutes, discussing what little they knew and how they might help once they knew more, both long- and short-term.

Cancer. Mason couldn't even imagine. Could there be a scarier word for a parent to hear in relation to their child? Movement from Ginny's corner caught his eye. The girl rose, went to the door, and looked out. She returned to her chair with a loud huff of breath, sat heavily, and pulled the book back into her lap.

Jesse and her friends had tried to pull the reclusive Ginny into their circle on more than one occasion. Each time, the girl had thanked them politely, refusing to budge from her seat, her glance returning hopefully to the door like an eager toddler waiting to be picked up from a strange nursery school. It must be hard to be thrust into this situation with only strangers for company.

Mason went back to his drink. He didn't mind that it was cold. Coffee was comforting hot, but with cream and sugar, fine at any temperature.

A rattle and shake drew his attention back to the girl. He watched as she frowned at the drink cup she held, set it on the table, and retrieved her bag. She rummaged for a few seconds before pulling out a wallet. She looked inside, closed her eyes, and replaced it.

He walked closer. "Something wrong?"

Ginny looked up at him. "I'm just bored and my cup is empty. I thought about finding a vending machine, but all I have is a twenty."

Mason frowned into his cup. "This has pretty much served its purpose as well. I have a pocket full of change. Tell me what you want, and I'll get it for you."

She stood. "If you'll point me in the right direction, I'm sure there's a change machine close by."

"I don't mind," Mason said. "I'm going a little crazy too. If I go, you won't miss them when they come back."

The girl sent another look at the door. "You sure?"

"You'll be doing us both a favor." He held out a hand. "I'm Mason Saxton. A friend of your mother's. What can I get you?"

She accepted his hand, chewing her bottom lip as she looked up at him. "What I'd really like is some lemonade. I'm not much of a soda drinker." She waved at the large, empty cup. "That's my quota for the week."

"I'll see what I can find."

Mason returned ten minutes later with two bottles of lemonade, one yellow and one pink. Ginny looked up from her book when he stopped next to her chair. "Any word?"

"No."

"I'm sure it won't be much longer." He held up the bottles. "I wasn't sure which you preferred, regular or raspberry."

"That's sweet, but you didn't have to get both."

"I'll drink the other. Pick your poison."

"The raspberry then - if you're sure you like both."

Mason set the bottle of regular lemonade on the table and twisted the cap on the other. "Here you go." He motioned to the chair next to her. "Do you mind?"

When Ginny shrugged, he took the seat, opened his own drink, and glanced down at the open book. Not a book, an album full of pictures, striking pictures as far as his amateur eye could see. He leaned closer. "Did you take these?"

"Yeah." Ginny closed the cover and clasped her hands on top. "Mom and I were going to see about getting some of them framed this afternoon." The sigh Mason heard contained a fair share of discouragement. "Maybe in a few days."

Mason touched the edge of the album. "May I?"

Ginny shrugged and passed it over.

Mason spent a few minutes paging through the photos. He looked up about halfway through. "These are very good. You have a unique touch with lighting and balance."

She tilted her head. "You know photography?"

"I dabble. There's something very rewarding about getting the right shot."

Ginny sat straighter and turned toward him. "There is, isn't there? It's like you're just walking along and you stumble across this special little gift. Then, not only did you see something in that perfect instant, but you get to keep it forever."

"I never thought of it that way, but you're exactly right." Mason flipped a few more pages. "You have quite a gift."

He looked up and found Ginny's gaze on him. "I have a lot to learn. Can I show you something?"

Mason handed the book back to her. "Absolutely."

Ginny took it and flipped to the very back. "Grams and Gramps took me to Arches National Park last year."

"In Utah."

"You've been there?"

"A couple of times. It's a great place to take sunset shots. All that red rock against a bowl of blue sky. I've got one in the winter where the sky is streaked with purple and orange and the rocks are dusted with snow. Pretty amazing stuff."

Ginny nodded and handed the book back. "Take a look at these."

Mason studied the half dozen photos mounted on the last page of the book. In the most prominent, spears of rust-colored earth jutted up into a clear azure sky just darkening to dusk. A perfect round moon seemed to balance on the tip of one of the stone fingers as if trying to decide which way to fall. "Incredible."

"You don't see anything wrong with it?"

Mason bent for a closer look. He flipped back to her close ups, studied a few of those, then went back to the final photos. In the close ups, the subject was sharp and clear. In the landscape shots, things were just a bit out of focus. "You've got F-stop problems."

"I know, I dialed it in as tight as I could, and they just got worse. I was working my way back up, and I lost the light."

"You were headed in the right direction. And these are still great shots." He closed the book and handed it back. "You know, my camera is out in the car. Why don't I go get it? I can show you while we wait."

"That would be awesome!"

"I'll be right back." Mason stood. "Ladies, I'm going out to the car for a few minutes. Can I get anyone anything?"

Jesse looked up. "I'm fine, Dad." The other women responded in the negative as well.

"You guys want something interesting to do to pass the time? Let this young lady show you her photos. We are sitting in the midst of some serious talent." He left as the women motioned for Ginny to join them. He paused in the hall, looking up and down, hoping to see Syd. No such luck. He punched the button for the elevator.

Father, please be with them now. Give them Your peace in this storm.

Syd had seemed genuinely happy to see him earlier. If the roadblocks in their friendship truly revolved around the reappearance of Ginny, maybe God had just opened a door for him. He'd tread lightly there, of course. He remembered the mess Garrett had gotten into last fall with that girl from his school. But Mason had something in common with Ginny, something he could help her with. If Ginny saw him as a friend, Maybe Syd would thaw out a little more.

CHAPTER 14

*C*harley looked at Ginny. "Kinsley told me your pictures were good, but these are way beyond that."

Ginny smiled at her friend's mother. "Kinsley's are just as good."

"Kinsley has talent, but for her, photography is a hobby. I see career in these."

"You should set up a website and post some of these for sale," Mac told her. "I can put you in touch with the person who designed the site for the spa. He does really good work."

Ginny considered. "Mom mentioned maybe selling some through the bookstore. I never thought of getting a website of my own."

"You should." Mom's boss, Randy, tapped a manicured nail on a photo of a mama giraffe nuzzling her baby. "And when you do, I want one of these for Astor's room. She's about outgrown the baby decorations, and she loves giraffes. If this can be enlarged to poster size, we could do the whole room around it."

"It'll enlarge just fine."

Alex pulled the book from Randy's grasp. "And I want these three for my office," she said. "Yellow roses are my favorite."

Jesse held up a hand. "Y'all back off. My father-in-law turned us onto this young lady. It's my turn." She took procession and flipped through to a picture of a butterfly, its translucent wings outlined in black, nestled into a bouquet of pink flowers. "I want this one. Something I can put in my tiny office to remind me that life exists on the outside."

Ginny shook her head. These women were out of control. She didn't know whether to be flattered or afraid.

"How much for an eight-by-ten of the butterfly?" Jesse persisted.

"I...umm...never thought about it."

"Well, it's time to think about it," Mac said. "I'm going to want some framed enlargements for the nursery. And you make those prices fair for you. No skimping allowed."

"I'll be sure and get back to you with..." Her words tapered off as Mom stepped into the room. Ginny scrambled to her feet, the album clutched to her chest like a shield. Mom looked haggard. Her eyes were puffy and red, and there were smudges of mascara on her cheeks. She stopped just inside the door and held out a hand. Ginny hurried across the room to take it.

"Mom?" She didn't pull away when Mom pulled her into her arms. "Is Logan OK?"

"He's sleeping." She pulled back a bit and looked into Ginny's eyes. "Sweetheart, I'm so sorry about leaving you out here for so long. We weren't ignoring you. Logan was so groggy when we first went back. Then we had to talk to his doctor, and now he's sleeping. They have a strict two visitor rule, but I promise I'll come get you for a visit as soon as he wakes up."

"You were gone so long, I was really worried."

"We all were," Randy said. "What have they told you?"

Ginny shifted to her mom's side but kept hold of her hand while Mom talked to her friends.

"Not a lot," her mom said. "It looks like he's spending the

night. You guys should probably go home. I'll call you once we have anything to share."

"You won't get rid of us that easily," Alex said.

"Yeah." Mac reclaimed her seat in one of the vinyl chairs. "I'm just starting to get comfortable."

Randy crossed her arms. "I'm not going anywhere."

"Ditto," Charley said.

"You're stuck with us," Jesse plopped down on one of the sofas. "Friends don't let friends wait alone. You go on back and be with Sara and Logan. We'll hold the fort here."

"You guys are the best," Mom whispered. Her gaze swept the room. "Did Mason leave?"

"Your friend went out to his car for a minute," Ginny told her. "He should be right back."

Mom nodded. "Give him an update for me and try to make him go home."

"Yeah, that'll happen," Jesse said from her place on the couch. She made a motion with her hands. "Shoo...we've got this."

Mom pulled Ginny close a second time. "It means so much that you're here."

For the first time, Ginny was glad she was in Oklahoma. The wait was making her a little nuts, but she'd be certifiable waiting for word three states away. It had been a long time since Ginny had felt so connected to her mom and her sister. She despised the circumstances but appreciated the feeling. She hugged her mom back. "I'm glad I am. I'm sorry I've been such a pain."

Mom took a step back and cupped Ginny's face in her hands. "None of that right now. For now—"

"You need to get back to Sara and Logan. I'm not going anywhere." Ginny watched her mom walk away with fresh tears in her eyes. She wasn't worried about the tears. Sometimes tears were a good place to start. Her phone vibrated in her pocket, and she pulled it free.

Avery. About time. He hadn't called her on Sunday. Hadn't returned one of the dozen calls or texts she'd sent in the last three days.

Ginny stepped out into the hall and swiped the call open. "Avery, where have you been?"

"Hey, Gin. I thought I should return your calls before your messages blew up my phone."

"Ha-ha." But there was something in the tone of his voice that made her pause mid-stride.

"So, what's up?" he asked.

What's up? They hadn't seen each other in almost a week, hadn't talked either, and all he had to say was *what's up?* "I just miss you is all."

"Oh, yeah. Uh, about that… We need to talk."

The words spiked Ginny's pulse and sent it pounding in her ears. She stopped walking and leaned a shoulder against the wall. "What?"

"I just…well…"

Ginny could almost picture him running his hands through his mop of red hair before pushing his glasses back into place.

"I just don't think…I mean, I'm sorry, but I don't think we should talk anymore."

Heat started at Ginny toenails and worked its way up her entire body. "You're breaking up with me…over the phone?" Her voice rose sharply on the last word.

"Yeah, well, you're a thousand miles away, so… Besides, I wouldn't actually call it breaking up. We went out a couple of times. I just, you know… I've got a life. The whole long-distance thing doesn't work."

"But…" Ginny snapped her mouth shut. Now the unreturned texts and unanswered calls made sense, and she had more pride than to argue about it, even on a day like today. Especially on a day like today. "Fine. See ya." She swiped the call closed and bolted for the red exit sign. She was going to bawl, and she wasn't going to do it in front of a bunch of strangers.

Ginny burst out of the door on the ground level, tears hot on her cheeks. She blinked in the sudden light, bowed her head, and hugged her arms around herself. Dumped, by phone. Could her week get any worse? Gramps's heart attack, ripped from home and slammed into Oklahoma, her nephew probably had cancer, and Avery...

Ginny allowed her eyes to focus on the sky. "This is Your fault," she whispered to God. She'd lied to her mom and Sara about the whole God thing. Her grandparents had tried to teach her to trust, and there hadn't been a time when she'd been allowed to stay out of church, but all the church services in the world weren't enough to keep a person believing when every prayer you ever prayed bounced off a brick wall of nothing.

"Nothing, that's all I've ever gotten out of You. But I'll give You one thing. At least You're consistent." Her conscience tugged, and she pushed it out of the way. "You've ruined my life. I begged to come home and got nothing. I got comfortable and begged to stay, a bunch more nothing. There's only one innocent person in this whole eight-year mess, and now You're picking on him. And Avery..." Ginny knew it was wrong, but she needed someone to blame, and God in all His manipulating, omnipotent, chess piece welding ways was the perfect One. "Can't You just leave us alone?"

The words broke something free in Ginny's heart and her tears poured like a torrent down her cheeks. She dashed at her eyes with the sleeve of her shirt. "You're up there just watching all this happen. Don't you care what You're doing to us, even just a little?"

"Ginny?"

It didn't matter that she hardly knew him. All that mattered was that she needed a life preserver in a current that threatened to suck her under. She turned and launched herself into Mason Saxton's arms.

* * *

HIS ARMS CLOSED around her out of reflex. "Hey now, what's all this?" he asked as she clung to him. He glanced up at the building, his own heart clenched in a tight fist.

Logan.

"Is it Logan? Was there word?"

Sobs wracked her whole body. She blubbered through the tears, but he couldn't understand a thing she said. He patted her back. Poor kid, what else could it be? Mason closed his eyes. *Jesus, just be with them.* "I'm so sorry, Ginny." He spotted a bench a few steps off the path. "Here, come with me."

Mason led her to the bench and pulled her down beside him. He dug his handkerchief—still clean, thank God—from his pocket and pressed it into her hands. He rested one arm on the back of the bench, giving her what comfort he could while she cried herself out. Once the child's crying dwindled, he shifted to face her, took the square of linen from her fingers, and dabbed at her face.

She took it from him and finished the job with a hefty blow of her nose. She folded the square, held it out to him, then yanked it back as red colored her cheeks. "Sorry. I'll make sure it gets washed, and Mom can get it back to you."

"That's fine. Are you better now? Maybe we should go back in. I'm sure your mom and sister need you with them just now."

The girl's brow furrowed. "Mom and Sara? They don't know..." She glanced at the building. "Oh..."

Mason studied her. Had he misunderstood? "This wasn't about your nephew?"

"Yes...no..." The handkerchief came back out and Ginny

wiped her eyes. "Not entirely. I, um…" She pulled the phone from her pocket. "I got some bad news from a friend, and it was just…" She looked away and her lower lip trembled. "It was too much on top of everything else. I came out here to get some air." She brought her gaze back to his. "Sorry if I scared you."

He shifted his arm to give her shoulders a squeeze. "You've got a lot on your mind right now. A meltdown along the way is understandable."

"You don't know the half of it."

He caught the mumbled words and cocked his head. Oh, how he longed to ask what she meant. Despite her earlier reaction to his presence, Syd certainly wasn't providing many answers. But as appealing an opportunity as this might be, he wouldn't grill her daughter for answers Syd needed to share.

"Are you a Christian?" Ginny asked.

The leftfield question startled him. It took him a second to catch up and switch gears. "I am, but I'm still new at it. You?"

"Not so much." She glanced up at the hospital building and then down at the phone clutched in one of her hands. Her words continued almost as if she were speaking to herself more than him. "They tell you how much God loves you and wants nothing but the best for you, that He wants to be your Father and stuff. But he took my dad away, and Donny…" The shoulders under Mason's arm shuddered. "Not going there. Gramps was sort of like my dad, and now Gramps is sick, too." Her lips pursed in concentration. "Now Logan might die…" Her words trailed off as she gave the fear a voice. She bounced the phone in her palm. "And now this? How can anyone believe when there's so much evidence against it?"

What could Mason say to this troubled child? Then he remembered a verse in the Psalms that he'd shared with Garrett during that mess his son had endured last winter. "Ginny, I know that there are times when it seems like God must be asleep. The disciples who walked with Jesus and shared in His miracles had doubts when the storm threatened to sink their boat. But there's a verse." He took out his phone, opened an app, and tapped the screen a few times. "Here it is. Psalm nine, verse ten. 'And they that know thy name will put their trust in thee: for thou Lord, hast not forsaken them that seek you.'" He put his phone away and returned his arm to the youngster's shoulders.

"I know it's hard to trust God's plan when it messes with what we think our life should look like. Even though I haven't been a Christian for long, I'm learning that He sees more than I can, and He has a purpose for things I don't always understand. Can I pray with you?"

The slim shoulders under his arm lifted in a small shrug. Mason took that as a yes and closed his eyes. "Jesus, we need Your help. First of all, be with Logan. We're all afraid…" He paused when a sob escaped Ginny, and her head fell to his shoulder. Mason gave her a little squeeze and leaned his head against hers. "We need You to bring healing for him and peace for those who love him. After that, could You give Ginny an extra hug today? She's feeling a little lost and needs to be reminded of how much You love her. Wrap her in Your arms and remind her that she's never been alone, even when the situation was hard to understand."

He finished and sat quietly while Ginny collected herself. When she finally straightened and wiped her eyes, he studied her. "Better?"

"Maybe a little."

"I'll make a deal with you."

She tilted her head in question.

"I'll keep praying if you'll keep seeking."

"I can do that."

"Good." Mason stood and pulled her to her feet. "Let's get back inside and see if there's any news." He patted the nearly forgotten camera case that hung from one shoulder. "I can still show you the correct setting for your camera if you're interested."

"I'd like that." Ginny started back into the building. She stopped when Mason's phone rang.

He motioned her ahead. "I need to take this. Go on up. I'll be there shortly."

CHAPTER 15

*S*ara paced the small hospital room. Each time she passed the clock she sent a malicious glare in its direction as if the force of her agitation could do something to make the hands on the thing move faster. She wanted a report on her child, and she wanted it yesterday.

Logan turned over, and a soft groan whispered from his lips. Picturing the needle jabbed into his hip bone, she rushed to the rail and brushed the hair off her baby's forehead. Despite the picture painted by her vivid imagination, her son slept soundly, whether from the drugs in his system or exhaustion. Sara didn't care. His skin was dry and cool, and he'd kept his dinner down.

When the door opened, Sara looked up, her hopes plummeting when her mom came into the room instead of the doctor she was hoping for.

"Any news?" Mom asked.

She shook her head and looked again at Logan. "I'm going out of my mind. How much trouble is it to read some lab results?"

"I know, sweetheart. I have to keep reminding myself that we aren't the only ones waiting for news. This place is filled with anxious parents and grandparents. They aren't keeping news from us intentionally."

"I wish I had your grace." Sara crossed her arms around herself and rubbed the fabric of the long sleeved T-shirt as her mother stood on the other side of the bed.

"You cold?" Mom asked.

"No, just..." Sara paced away. "I don't really know what I am. Helpless maybe. I don't like it." She crossed to the window and stared down at the ground. From this room on the fourth floor, she had a nice view of the manicured grounds. Trees, smooth lawns, tidy sidewalks, and pots of colorful fall flowers, placed along wide walkways. The hospital went to a lot of trouble to make their patients and families comfortable. A few adults walked along the sidewalks pushing IV poles or wheelchairs for small patients, taking advantage of the warm temperatures and the soft light of the early September day. In a couple of weeks, daylight savings time would end and it would be dark by this time of the evening.

She frowned as a familiar figure exited the building. She cocked her head and watched as her sister paced up and down a stretch of sidewalk for several seconds before throwing herself into the arms of a man.

What? Sara blinked. She grew more confused as the two held each other for a moment before they moved to a bench and sat huddled together in an intimate conversation. The man's arm rested around Ginny's shoulders, and her sister seemed perfectly at home in his embrace. Something cold washed across Sara's heart and drew up a shudder of memory.

Donny?

But that was impossible, wasn't it? Sara closed her eyes. She had Donny on the brain thanks to Dr. Price's suggestion she reach out to Logan's father as a possible donor. She opened her eyes and peered through the fading light. Not Donny, but, even though she couldn't see either of them clearly, she could see enough to know that the guy was a man, not a boy. A boy would have been nothing but a curiosity, but a man...a much older man... Sara sucked in a breath as Ginny and the man's heads rested together while they talked like old and dear friends.

Who was it?

Ginny'd been in town less than a week.

Who was this guy, and why did he have his hands on her sister? The two questions liquefied the cold in Sara's heart and set it boiling. She would not stand idle and allow her sister to fall into the trap that had ensnared her.

She turned away from the window and looked at her mom watching Logan sleep. Love for the woman flooded her. There were times Sara didn't know how her mother had forgiven her for such betrayal, but she had. Forgiven and supported. She couldn't allow history to repeat itself.

"Mom, could you come over here?"

Mom came around the bed. "What do you need?"

Sara turned back to the window. "I need to show you—" They were gone.

Mom stood beside her, peering through the window. "What?"

Sara leaned closer to the glass, searching for Ginny and the stranger. She didn't see them. "I...I thought..." She looked at her mother. "Ginny was down there just now—"

"Probably just stretching her legs. We're all a little restless."

"With a guy."

"Oh." Mom turned back to the window. "Maybe she ran into someone from school."

"I don't think so."

"What do you mean?"

"Mom, it wasn't a boy, it was a man. An older man." Sara swallowed. "He..." Her arms came back around her chest as the unpleasant words stuck in her throat. "He had his hands all over her."

Mom's head snapped up, and she took a step back.

Sara took a deep breath and let it out slowly. "Ginny was down there with some man. They were wrapped up together like old friends…or something more."

Mom stared at her, one hand over her mouth, the other bunching the fabric of her shirt at her neck.

"Mom, I know you don't want to believe me. I don't want to believe me, but I know what I saw." Her eyes filled. "You asked me why I didn't come to you when Donny…" She swallowed back the rest of the sentence and the words she still couldn't say. "Why I didn't come to you. I'm coming to you now because I don't want the same thing that happened to me to happen to Ginny."

"But she wouldn't—"

Irritation replaced her fear. "I'm not making this up."

"Oh, Sara, of course you aren't. I just can't imagine Ginny putting any of us in that situation."

"Mom, don't brush this off. You need to find out what's going on."

A light knock sounded on the door a second before it was pushed open to admit Dr. Price. Sara studied his face, alarmed at the gravity of his expression. She reached for her mother's hand and held it. She bit her lip.

"I've just received word from the lab."

Sara closed her eyes and braced her heart for the worst.

"They're not going to have any results for you before morning. I'm sorry."

The breath left Sara's lungs in a whoosh. She heard a similar reaction from her mom.

She stared at the doctor.

"I know you're upset, I don't blame you," Dr. Price continued. "I know the waiting is the hardest part of the process."

Did he know though? Had he ever been through this?

"Will you both be spending the night?"

Sara looked at her mom.

"I need to check on Ginny."

Sara nodded and turned back to the doctor. "Me for sure."

"I'll have an additional recliner brought in, and I'll have the nurse arrange for two dinner trays, just in case. If you need anything else, just ring the nurse's station. I'll stop back by first thing in the morning."

* * *

SYD'S HEART and feet were leaden as she and Sara trudged back to the waiting room to deliver the information.

Her mind whirled. Did Logan have leukemia or didn't he? Was God still punishing her or wasn't He? And what about that silly cloth? She'd taken that as good news. And Ginny…Sara's concerns needed to be dealt with, but she didn't think she could do it right now. *Father, I don't know how much more I can take today.*

They stepped into the waiting room. Her friends and Ginny still waited, coming to their feet as they entered. Mason wasn't there. A part of Syd's heart was disappointed that he'd gone, but the man had a life, after all.

Ginny hurried to her mother's side. "Mom?"

Syd wrapped her arm around her daughter's back. "They aren't going to be able to tell us anything till sometime in the morning." Groans of protest circled the room.

Syd looked at her friends. "You guys… I can't tell you how much your being here has meant. But there's no reason for you to stay any longer tonight."

Syd looked at Ginny and swallowed against the racing of her heart. Her daughter was so beautiful, so young and fresh. *Oh God, I can't face this a second time.* Both of her daughters needed her right now, but she couldn't be in two places at once. Syd made a decision.

"Ginny, if you'll give me a few minutes, I'll be ready to go."

"Go where?"

"Home with you. I'll come back here after I take you to school in the morning."

"No," Ginny said. "You need to be here. I can…" She looked at Charley. "Mrs. Hubbard, could I come to your house?"

"Of course," Charley said. "I was about to volunteer."

Syd took Ginny's hand. "Are you sure?"

"Absolutely."

She looked at Charley. "I know it's an imposition, but—"

"You take that back." Charley put her hands on her hips and glared at Syd. "If I were standing in that doorway and Kinsley needed a place to stay in an emergency, would she be welcome at your house?"

"You know she would."

"Then why should you think I'd be different. I'll take Ginny by your house so she can get what she needs for tomorrow. She and Kinsley can have an old-fashioned sleepover."

Syd's sigh of relief was audible. "Thanks, Charley. Ginny, you good with that plan?"

"Yes." Ginny returned to her chair to gather her things. "But can I please see Logan before we leave? You promised."

"He's sleeping," Sara said, "but come with me and you can kiss him good night before you go."

"And I'll go with the girls," Charley said, holding out her arms. "Give me a hug now. We'll go straight out to the car from there." She pulled Syd close. "I know that this is pretty pointless advice, but try and get some sleep tonight. God's got this whole thing."

"I know." Syd sank into the hug. "Thanks for…everything."

"No problem." Charley let go of Syd and turned to Ginny. "Give me some of your things. I'll take care of it while you hug your mom and visit with Logan."

Ginny shifted the book bag and the album into Charley's arms and pulled her mom close. "Call me if there's any news."

"You know I will."

Syd sank into a chair as Sara led Ginny and Charley down the hall.

Alex squatted in front of her and took her hands. "How are you holding up?"

"I'm not really." Syd allowed her gaze to travel from one face to another. Alex and her delicate features, fully dressed in her *pastor's wife* hat for the time being. Randy, more than a boss right now. Jesse, her brown eyes full of compassion behind glasses that never seemed to stay in place. Mac, her dark brown hair pulled up into a high ponytail, just a trace of fatigue in the slouch of her shoulders. And Charley, absent from their gathering so she could do Syd a favor. Syd had never had friends like these…sisters really. Soeurs, the spa where they gathered three times a week, translated into sisters. Maybe it was just a fluke, but it was more than appropriate for the six of them.

"I'm trying to stay positive for Sara's sake." Syd's gaze darted to the hall and back. Sara wasn't on her way back yet so she continued, "But I'm scared to death."

"Oh honey, of course you are." Randy rubbed her shoulder.

"You wouldn't be human if you weren't," Jesse said.

"Is there anything we can do for you?" Mac asked. "Can we bring you guys dinner?"

Syd shook her head. "I know you guys are praying. That's what we need now. The doctor ordered us dinner trays, but I appreciate the offer."

A throat cleared from the door, and Syd looked up to see Mason.

Something fluttered in her heart. He hadn't gone home. Her eyes filled, and she held out a hand to him.

Mason stepped into the room, pulled Syd to her feet, and held her close. She just sank in. There was something so right about the way his arms wrapped around her. For a second, the tension lifted and Syd could breathe.

"Is there news?" he whispered.

"Not until tomorrow. I was just sending everyone home." She lifted her head enough to look into his eyes. "But I'm so glad you're still here."

"What are you doing?" The question came from the doorway, angry and shocked.

The two broke apart, and Syd faced Sara. Her daughter was visibly trembling.

"Sara, what's wrong?" Syd reached a hand out to her daughter.

"What's wrong?" Sara took a step into the room and faced her mother and Mason. "It was him."

"What are you—?"

"I can't believe this." Sara's words became shrill. "I told you I saw some guy with his hands all over Ginny, and here he is with his hands all over you."

The world around Syd short-circuited as Sara's words slammed into her. A glimpse of a dried up cloth flashed through her mind. She wanted to object, to reassure her daughter, but one look at Sara told Syd all she needed to know.

But Mason? Syd stared at him.

The pain of fresh betrayal nearly doubled her over. She'd done it again. Allowed her feelings for a man to come before her common sense. How could she be so stupid? Ginny was vulnerable right now, and Syd had practically thrown the two of them together. And Mason? He'd obviously twisted that to his advantage.

Darkness crowded Syd's vision until she thought she might be sick. Everything that had happened today, all the doubts, the ugly possibilities, the self-recriminations, and now Sara's accusations rolled into a tight ball in Syd's stomach. The weight threatened to bring her to her knees. She'd been a fool eight years ago, and she was still a fool. But that cloth, she'd thought... Bile clawed up her throat.

"Oh dear God...oh dear God. I can't do this again." Syd took a half dozen steps away before facing Mason. He actually had the nerve to look confused.

"How could you?"

"Sydney, I—"

"No! I won't allow it. How dare you take advantage of this situation to put your hands on my daughter?" Her hand flew to cover her mouth. "I invited you into my home." *Jesus, help me.*

Mason stood his ground. Not an iota of shame filled his expression. "I have no idea what you're talking about."

Syd pressed her lips together while her eyes overflowed. That innocent look on his face almost made her doubt, but she'd seen it before. She'd been taken in before. Her family couldn't take a second hit. Donny had almost destroyed them.

"I can't look at you." Heedless of the questions from her friends and the look of indignation on Mason's face, Syd bolted from the room with Sara on her heels.

CHAPTER 16

*M*ason stared after her. *What in the world?* He didn't even have words to form the questions he needed to ask.

A gentle touch on his arm pulled his attention away from the door. Jesse peered up at him, her confused expression mirrored his own.

"What was that all about?" she asked.

Mason put an arm around his daughter-in-law's shoulders. "No idea."

"Someone should go after her." Randy, the pretty redhead, sent a concerned glance to the corridor. "I've never seen her act like that. I think—"

"No..." Alex drew the word out. "Maybe we shouldn't."

Mac bit her lip. "She's really upset."

"That's an understatement." Jesse clasped her hands around one of Mason's arms. "I have no idea what she meant just now, but Mason doesn't deserve to take the brunt of her tirade. We need to talk to her."

Mason patted Jesse's hands. His little daughter-in-law could be a spitfire. He liked that about her.

"Yes, we do," Alex said. "But I don't think this is the time or place." She looked at Mason. "You do deserve an explanation, but I don't think now's the time to go looking for it." She too looked down the hall where they'd disappeared. "We all have a breaking point, and I think Syd just found hers. Going after her right now is only going to add weight to that." She returned her focus to Mason. "You can understand that, right?"

Mason wasn't sure that he understood anything. Not a thing Syd or her daughter had said made any sense. *His hands on her daughter*. Something happening *again*. All he was certain of was that he didn't like it.

He looked down at the diminutive Alex. She had a point. Syd had way too much on her plate just now. Whatever had caused her outburst, he doubted that anyone would get to the root of it tonight.

I can't do this again. Syd's words echoed in his ears and left a sour taste in Mason's mouth.

Again.

An idea took shape in his head. He wondered if the thing that couldn't happen again had left a cyber-trail the first time. Sara's last name was Marlin. Syd's was Patterson. He wasn't an investigator, but he could Google with the best of them. With a few more pieces to the puzzle, there might be a way to find some of the answers without dragging them out of Syd.

"You're right." He focused on Alex. "I don't think there's anything to be gained by pursuing this tonight. But could you ladies answer a couple of questions for me?"

"If we can," Jesse answered.

"Has Sara ever been married?"

The women looked at each other. "No." Randy tilted her head. "How does that help?"

He shrugged. "I was just curious about the difference in their last names. Sara Marlin, Sydney Patterson."

Randy answered, "Patterson was the name of Syd's second

husband. I don't remember his first name, don't know anything about him really. Syd doesn't talk about him. Anthony Marlin was her first husband." Randy narrowed her eyes. "Where are you going with this?"

"Just a hunch I want to look into. If you're uncomfortable giving me information, I won't hold it against you."

Randy looked around at the women and took a silent poll. She received shrugs and nods in response.

"Where did she live before Garfield?"

"Utah." Randy tapped a finger on her forehead. "Oh, what was the name of the town? Something Gun…Gunston…Gunsby…" She snapped her fingers. "Gunnison. Gunnison, Utah."

* * *

IN LOGAN'S ROOM, Syd lay on her cot, curled into a tight fetal position, her face to the wall. She was hollowed out, unable to cry, unable to pray, unable to think past the numbing cold wrapped around her. If breathing had required conscious thought, she would have died.

She'd been here before. The weekend Sara and Donny went missing. When she'd found the marijuana and the stack of delinquent notices hidden in the back of Donny's drawer. The night the sheriff came to the door with the paperwork to repossess the car. The night spent in darkness because Donny hadn't paid the electric bill. The night spent alone because Anthony's parents had taken Ginny. Blow stacked on blow, a weight too heavy to be borne. At least the emptiness was quiet and carried the assurance that things were bad but they couldn't get any worse. A sob escaped. How had she been chosen to visit the emptiness twice in her lifetime?

"Mom?"

"I'm OK. I just need to sleep." Her voice sounded as scraped out as the rest of her. And despite the emotional void she found herself in, there was still guilt. Sara needed her to be strong right now, and here she lay, unable...just unable. She dredged up a question. "Logan still sleeping?"

"Yes."

"Good. You should get some rest as well."

Eight years ago when she'd been trapped in the emptiness, at least she'd been alone. At least she'd had a few hours to pull herself together, to decide what came next. Maybe she could be strong tomorrow.

"OK," Sara told her, "but the nurse just delivered a note from your friends."

Syd didn't have a response as another weight settled on her heart. She wouldn't have any of those friends come morning.

Paper rustled, and then Sara read, "We love you and we're praying for you. Alex."

Nice, but when the truth came out, they'd be gone. And after the scene in the waiting room, the truth would come out. It was just a matter of time. They'd either be appalled at her past or, where Jesse was concerned, forced to choose between Syd and Mason. Syd would lose either way.

Mason.

His anguished face filled her mind. Confused, innocent... loving. Syd pushed it away. She had firsthand experience that those emotions could be feigned. She'd done what she had to do. She'd failed Sara, and they were still paying the price for her blindness. She wouldn't fail Ginny.

* * *

MASON UNLOCKED HIS FRONT DOOR, shoved it open, and met Brody's charge. He petted the dog. "I know, boy, I'll get your dinner right now." The dog danced around his feet while he poured food into the bowl and put out fresh water. While his hands were occupied with routine tasks, his mind replayed the scene in the waiting room. Syd had looked stricken, the older daughter indignant. He tried to twist it into something that made sense and failed.

Once the dog was taken care of Mason retreated to his study and booted up his computer. He paused with his fingers poised over the keyboard. Privacy was a gray area in today's cyberspace world, but digging into Syd's past felt like a violation in a lot of ways.

How dare you take advantage of this situation to put your hands on my daughter?

Syd's question rang in his ears, no more palatable now than it had been earlier. Something else rang in his ears as well.

Be her friend.

It certainly looked like that had failed. He deserved to know why, didn't he?

His mind made up, the room filled with the clacking of the keyboard. Finding the site for the Gunnison, Utah, paper was a fairly easy task. Mason navigated to the obituaries and typed in the name of Syd's first husband, Anthony Marlin.

The screen filled with the archived story and a picture of a handsome man in his early forties. He had a clean-shaven face, blond hair combed back from his forehead and temples, and a mouth split in laughter.

Mason studied the picture for several seconds. Both of Syd's girls had inherited this man's eyes. He leaned closer to the screen and read the words in a whisper. "Anthony Charles Marlin, age forty-one, passed from this life Tuesday evening. He leaves behind his wife, Sydney, and his daughters, Sara and Ginny. Services are pending." Mason shook his head while he scrolled through the article that covered Anthony's life and history. Sympathy for Syd and her young family flooded him. He knew the pain of losing a spouse, but couldn't imagine losing one so young.

Mason exited the obituaries and sat back. He had a last name for the second husband, but not a first. He stared at the screen for a few seconds before puzzlement gave way to an idea. He clicked on the archive button, navigated to the public notice section and typed in Syd's name. An application for a marriage license popped up. The groom was Donny Patterson.

I've got you now.

Mason went back to the archives and typed in Donny Patterson. This time the screen filled with a series of headlines listed by date. Mason clicked on the first one and began to read.

Donny Royce Patterson, age thirty-two, was arrested last night and charged with one count of abduction and rape of an unnamed fifteen-year-old female.

The words knocked Mason back into his seat. He narrowed his eyes at the screen but his brain was doing the math. The date on the article was seven and a half years ago.

An unnamed fifteen-year-old girl.

A baby born to a sixteen-year-old.

An ex-husband accused of rape.

Mason inhaled a sharp breath and his hands clenched on the keyboard.

This is what Syd's accusing me of.

How could she think such a thing? Mason shoved away from the desk, too agitated to finish reading the rest of the articles.

He paced the small room. Of all the things Mason had expected his move to Garfield to bring, being accused of such a vile act hadn't been anywhere on the list.

Be her friend.

The quiet, repetitive words stopped him cold, and he turned his focus inward, sure he'd heard wrong. *You're kidding, right? There is no way I can have a relationship with this woman. What if she takes this harebrained accusation to the cops?*

When the initial burst of nervous energy passed Mason returned to the computer and scrolled through the rest of the stories. The words sickened him and split his heart down the middle. Part of him wanted to find Syd and offer her the comfort she obviously still needed. Part of him was repulsed to be lumped into the same category as Donny Patterson.

His hands on her daughter. The words made more sense now, but he'd been tackled and used as a crying pillow. He hadn't... He shut the down computer with a sharp jab to the button. A man's integrity was sacred. He'd done nothing to violate his, regardless of what Syd might think. If she thought him capable of... He searched for words and couldn't find them. If that was the sort of man she thought he was, their friendship was over.

CHAPTER 17

*S*yd sat on her cot in Logan's room Thursday morning and picked at her breakfast tray. She'd barely slept, her dreams haunted with images of Donny and Sara, their faces morphing into Mason's and Ginny's. Every time she'd jerked to consciousness, the broken pieces of her heart had ground together like glass in a meat grinder.

She'd tried to focus less on her own stupidity and more on thanking God that she'd seen the truth of Mason's intentions before it went too far. Those prayers gave her no comfort. Visions of that wet-turned-dry cloth haunted her and added to her confusion. What had it all meant, and how had she gotten it so wrong? She tried to find peace in doing the right thing this time, but peace escaped her. Instead, her heart ached with a nagging disquiet.

She'd tried and failed to connect with Ginny this morning. Every call went straight to her daughter's voicemail. Each missed call drove panic a bit deeper into Syd's heart. What was going on? Syd rubbed her forehead, torn in half with impossible decisions. She needed to be with Ginny right now, needed to get to the bottom of what Sara saw, but she couldn't leave

Sara and Logan. If the doctor brought bad news, they'd need her.

Jesus, show me what to do.

Across the room, Logan and Sara sat on the side of the big bed and ate and laughed. Logan seemed much improved this morning, which should have helped Syd's mental state, but too many unanswered questions hovered just out of reach. Syd could see the hooded worry in her daughter's eyes and knew it mirrored her own.

The memory of that wet-dry cloth floated into her mind once more. Syd pushed that failed experiment away. Yes, she'd enjoyed her time with Mason, but her heart had been trying to warn her for days. She should have listened. Instead, she'd almost put her family in harm's way a second time. *Selfish, selfish, selfish.*

"Grandma, look." Logan held up a partially eaten piece of toast. The boy made growling noises. "I made a monster."

If Syd twisted her head just right, it looked a little like a bear. Her lips quirked up. She loved this child. In the face of all the worry, he brought joy. "You better eat him before he eats you."

Logan grinned and took a ferocious bite. "I chomped his head off!" A spasm of giggles had Logan rolling on the bed and Sara grabbing to steady the trays.

The door opened, and Dr. Price peeked into the room. "Now there's a sound I don't hear often enough. A satisfied customer."

Logan sat up, his eyes suddenly wary. He scooted behind his mother as if to hide himself from a threat. Syd could almost feel sorry for this man who obviously loved kids but had to cause them pain to bring healing.

"I see you back there," he told Logan. "You ready to go home?"

"Home?" Syd and Sara voiced the word at the same time.

"It is with great delight and relief that I am giving Logan a clean bill of health." He paused. "Clean except for a bad case of mononucleosis."

Sara pushed to her feet. "Mono...? But you said..."

Dr. Price folded his hands behind his back. "Dr. Hernandez did a mono spot test with the initial round of lab work. It came back negative, but Logan's platelet count was abnormally low, one of the things we look for in diagnosing leukemia. Regardless of the cause, low platelets can cause death if the decline continues. It's not something we can ignore. We had to take precautions until we got to the bottom of it."

"I still don't get it," Sara said. "I mean, I'm thrilled, but on Tuesday he didn't have mono, but on Thursday he does?"

"On Tuesday, the mono spot was negative, but in the time between then and now, his lab work showed a marked increase in his mono serum titers. Sometimes it takes an extra day or two for the levels of heterophile antibodies in a patient's blood to become detectable. But it was a day or two where we couldn't ignore the very real threat of leukemia."

The doctor looked at Logan, who'd come out from behind his mother and was looking perplexed by all the medical talk. "Lots of big words to say Logan can go home. We'll get him a mild pain reliever for the achy muscles and something for his other symptoms."

"But what about the throwing up?" Sara asked. "That's not a mono symptom, is it?"

"Not normally. I've looked at his chart from his last visit with Dr. Joe. He mentioned prescribing something for a stomach bug." The doctor sent a pointed look at Logan's breakfast plate, all but licked clean. "He can have that as prescribed, but somehow, I don't think you'll need it. Any other questions?"

"School?" Sara asked.

"Plan to keep him home for the rest of this week and next. Schedule him in to see Dr. Joe at the end of next week. If everything looks good, he should be good to go back at that time."

He looked down at Logan. "I'm going to get a pretty nurse in here to take that needle out of your arm, and then you can leave."

"Yay!" Logan fell back on the bed, kicked his feet in delight, and reached for his knee. "Ouch."

The doctor grinned at him. "Yep, you're gonna be achy for a while longer, but you'll get over it."

* * *

SYD LISTENED to the ringing phone before her boss answered. "Miranda Page."

"It's me."

"You have news?" The question was full of anxiety.

"Good news." Syd filled her friend and boss in on the doctor's diagnosis. "I'm going to need a couple of days off to help take care of Logan. Sara's job is so new, she doesn't have a lot of paid days she can take—"

"Just tell me what you need," Randy said. "You have a very generous boss."

"Thanks. Sara's boss is being very flexible with her as well. We sort of thought if we took turns, no one would get too far behind. I'll be in tomorrow, but I need Tuesday and Thursday of next week off. If all goes well Logan should be cleared to go back to school after next Friday."

"Whatever you need to do works for me. I know you have to be walking on air right now. God is so good."

Syd closed her eyes and waited for the peace that a positive outcome should have produced. Instead, the emptiness pulled at her like waves lapping at the shore. "Yes." She sighed. "He's good, better than I deserve."

"About last night—"

"Not now, OK?" Syd felt the sting of fresh tears. "I know you guys love me." *At least they will until they know what an idiot I really am.* "And I will explain." She swallowed before she continued, "But for now can you just pass the word along to everyone. I promise I'll be at the spa in the morning. We'll talk then."

A few beats of silence passed. "You know I'm praying for you, right?"

An incoming call beeped in her ear, and Syd almost sighed with relief when she saw Ginny's number. "I'll talk to you tomorrow. Ginny's calling." Syd swiped the call closed and connected the other.

"Mom, I'm sorry I missed your calls. I turned my ringer off last night when I went in to say good-night to Logan. Please tell me there's news."

The simple explanation flooded Syd with relief. "The best, sweetheart." Syd relayed the news a second time.

"That's...that's... Oh my gosh. He's really OK?"

"He will be in a week or so."

"Can I see him? When are you guys coming home?"

"We're getting ready to leave now. We should be home by lunchtime. Why don't I come get you once I drop Sara and Logan off? I'll take you over there. We shouldn't stay long, but I'm sure Logan would love to see his auntie Ginny for a minute. Then we can have lunch together." Syd hesitated. "We need to talk."

"I have a better idea," Ginny said. "I know you must be tried. Why don't I have Kinsley bring me home at lunchtime? We can eat, take a short nap, and then go see Sara and Logan tonight."

"Are you sure you want to wait?"

"Mom, everyone's wrung out. I understand that."

"You're a good girl, Ginny. I'll see you in a bit."

"Love you."

"I love you—"

A beep sounded and the phone went dead in Syd's hand. She rubbed her temples where a headache threatened. Even with the good news about Logan, the final task of the day piled onto Syd's shoulders with a tangible weight. Ginny had sounded so happy and upbeat. There'd been no worry or hesitation from Ginny at the mention of their having a conversation. Surely if Mason had made an inappropriate advance to her, there would

be a telltale sign in her voice. She'd need some reassurance…
wouldn't she?

*Don't be stupid. You missed every sign eight years ago. Don't drag
another child through the mud of your selfishness.*

Syd cringed at the voice of her self-recriminations, and her
resolve hardened. She wouldn't make the same mistake twice.

* * *

"Mom."

The front door slammed with a bang that echoed through
the house.

"Mom, guess what." Ginny stared down at the paper in her
hand. They wanted her…her! She was so excited, she was about
to explode.

"What in the world are you doing?" Mom came out of the
kitchen, wiping her hands on a towel. "You almost had to eat
your salad off the floor."

Ginny danced across the room and put her hands on her
mother's shoulders. "Guess! You have to guess."

"Come sit down and tell me because I don't have a clue."

Ginny linked arms with her mother's and pulled her to the
table. She leaned over and spread out the paper. "They want me…
me and some of my pictures."

"Who—?"

"The bookstore. I told Kinsley about the job at the bookstore,
and we went by there just now. I talked to them, told them
working at a bookstore was my dream job. I probably sounded
like a book geek or something, but they gave me the job. Said the
application was just a formality. I start on Monday, right after
school. They want me to work Monday, Tuesday, Thursday and
every other Saturday. Can you believe it?"

Mom put her arms around her and hugged her hard. "I'm so
proud and happy for you."

Ginny cocked her head. Something in her mother's voice didn't sound so proud and happy. She shrugged it off. Mom was probably just tired. The last couple of days had been the worst. Ginny sat down and forked up a huge bite of salad. "Guess what else?"

Mom sat across from her and bowed her head before picking up her fork.

"Oh, sorry." Ginny laid the fork down and bowed her own head, almost bouncing in the chair with impatience. When she heard her mother's whispered "amen" she looked up. "Guess what else?"

"Sweetheart, my brain is jelly. You're just going to have to tell me."

Ginny chewed and swallowed. "I still had my album with me from yesterday, so I showed it to them and told them about your idea. They want some of my pictures too. I can't believe it. I have a job, they want to buy some of my photos, and your friends almost mauled me over the album yesterday. I may not even need you to pay half on the car." She shoved her barely touched lunch aside. "When can we look at cars? I'm a working woman now. I need wheels."

"How's tomorrow afternoon? I'll pick you up after school and take you back to the bank. You can look through the lot while I wrap things up in the office."

"Perfect. Can I hang out with Kinsley tonight? Your friend told me what I was doing wrong with some of my landscape shots. I can't wait to see if it works. We're going to take our cameras to the park and experiment."

"I guess. We won't stay long at Sara's. Which one of my friends knows about cameras?"

"Mason, he…"

Mom's fork clattered into her bowl. "Oh, Ginny." Tears tracked her mother's cheeks. "I'm so sorry."

Ginny sat back. What in the world? "What are you sorry about?"

"I'm sorry about Mason. Sorry he bothered you. It won't happen again."

Mason? He was a sweetheart. He hadn't *bothered* her. He'd pointed her in the right direction where her photography was concerned.

Mom got up, pulled her chair close, and took Ginny's hands. "This is what I wanted to talk about. I would have eased into it, but since you brought him up I want you to know that I understand how uncomfortable he must have made you feel. It won't happen again."

"I have no idea what you're taking about."

"It's OK, sweetheart. You can be honest with me. Sara saw him..." Mom looked away as if searching for the right word. "Sara saw him with his arms around you."

Ginny straightened, pushed back in her chair.

"She wasn't tattling, baby," Mom said, "she just doesn't want you to face what she had to face. I told Mason to stay away from us. I wish I'd paid more attention to Sara and Donny. I can't change the past, but I can protect your future."

Ginny stared at her mother. *Sara and Donny?* She drew in a sharp breath. "You think Mason is like Donny?"

"Sara said she saw him touching you."

Ginny shook her head. "No...oh, Mom."

"I know this is hard, but we have to talk about this. Did he... Did he touch you?" Mom's voice was soft, almost coaxing. "It almost sounds like you're taking up for him."

"I am." The words were a whisper. Ginny closed her eyes and bowed her head until her forehead rested against her mother's. She told her Mom about how she'd felt left out, about Mason's interest in her photos, and about his offer to help. "Then Avery..." Tears dotted their joined hands as she told Mom about the phone breakup and her argument with God.

"Mason didn't touch me, not like you think. I practically jumped into his arms. He had to hold onto me to keep both of us from ending up on the ground. He let me cry, and then he sat with me until I got myself together. He even…he even talked to me about God and how I might be jumping to the wrong conclusions. Mom, he prayed with me. I won't say that I had some sort of religious experience, but he made me think." She raised her head and looked her mother in the eye. "If Sara saw anything, she saw him praying. The whole thing with Donny wrecked our family. I swear I'd tell you if he did anything wrong."

Her mom's gaze locked on to hers for several long seconds before her eyes filled with tears.

"Mom, don't cry, I'm fine, I promise."

Her mom looked down at their joined hands and gave Ginny's a squeeze. "You know I love you, right?"

Ginny nodded. "I love you back. Please tell me you believe me about Mason."

Mom bit her lips, but the smile still trembled. "I believe you."

Ginny didn't think she'd ever heard three words spoken with such anguish.

CHAPTER 18

*S*yd rose early Friday morning. She bypassed her workout clothes and dressed for her day at the bank. Her friends didn't know it yet, but there wouldn't be a workout this morning. For her, there probably never would be again, not after she said what she was going there to say.

She'd promised Randy that she'd explain everything and, until yesterday afternoon, she'd been ready to give them the whole vicious truth. A truth filled with enough righteous indignation at a second betrayal that maybe, just maybe, they'd overlook her stupidity eight years ago in their rush to support her now, even if the man doing the betraying was close to their circle.

But now? Guilt over her wrong conclusions weighed on her every thought and left her weak. She'd been a fool, and not for any of the reasons she'd have listed the day before. She'd blamed her rash outburst on the stress of the moment, she'd tried to figure out a way to make it Donny's fault, she'd been tempted to blame Sara, and she'd tried to renew blame on Mason. Nothing worked. There was no spin to the story that made her ugly and false accusations easier to swallow. God had tried to give her someone to lean on, and Syd had let fear of Donny and the hurt he'd caused overrule her faith.

Father, forgive me. Help me grow in my trust of You.

There'd been such innocent confusion in Mason's eyes before she'd fled the room. As much as she longed to go back to bed and pull the blankets over her head, her conscience wouldn't allow her to ignore what she'd done. Syd grabbed her purse and straightened her shoulders. First she'd give her friends the explanation they wanted, and then Mason deserved a personal apology. She had no illusions about the state of their relationship, now or in the future. She'd driven that dagger deep on Wednesday. But she would set the record straight with him.

Today.

Syd parked in front of the spa. The line of cars at the curb told her that everyone else was already up there. She sat for a few moments to order her thoughts. There was a lot of ground to cover—painful, rocky ground. A lot of it she'd never tried to put into words outside her own head. She needed all of those words today. "Please, Father, just let me get through this with some shred of dignity."

Her feet were heavy on the stairs, and the steps seemed to have doubled in number. She reached for the knob and paused when laughter filtered through the door. Syd swallowed back tears. She was going to miss that sound, that sisterhood. *Father, I can't do this without You.*

The room fell silent when Syd stepped in.

Randy tilted her head and looked Syd up and down. "Not working out?"

"No." Syd hitched up her slacks and took her place on the floor, Alex on one side, Randy on the other. Charley and Mac watched her expectantly. Jesse had yet to look her way. "We need to talk." Syd licked her dry lips as every word she'd rehearsed evaporated from her brain. "I... There's some things..." She looked down when Alex laid a hand on her arm then back up into Alex's serious brown eyes.

"We're here for you. Whatever's got you so twisted up, you need to get it off your chest."

Charley leaned across the space and patted Syd's knee. "We've all been where you are for one reason or another. Let us help you."

Her friend's simple words of support threatened to undo Syd. "Thanks." She looked down at the colorful mats, swallowed the tears she refused to give in to, and started at the beginning.

"My first marriage was a fairy tale while it lasted. Anthony Marlin was everything good that a man can be." Syd bowed her head, flooded with memories of all she'd lost. "My second one was a six-month long nightmare."

"You told us Anthony had a stroke?" Mac prompted.

Syd nodded, gathered herself, and continued, "Yeah. At forty-one he was gone." She snapped her fingers. "Just that fast. No warning, no time to prepare, no chance for good-byes." She looked around. "Who plans for that? Husbands and fathers aren't supposed to die that young. If I told you I was lost at that point, you'd probably think you understood, but you wouldn't, not really."

"Sounds like he spoiled you," Randy said.

"In more ways than I could list." Syd drew in a couple of ragged breaths. She could spend the day talking about Anthony and how wonderful he'd been, but that wasn't what her friends needed to know.

"Take a breath." Alex got to her feet. "Anyone else need a bottle of water?"

"Please." Syd picked at the chipped polish on her nails and didn't continue until Alex came back to her spot. Plastic crackled as the lids were twisted from the bottles. Syd took a couple of deep swallows before she continued.

"As lost as we were, the girls and I managed. Anthony had a

decent life insurance policy. Not a fortune, but enough that I could still pay the bills without working as long as I was careful. I was so grateful for that. The girls needed me more than ever, and I needed them just as much. We'd probably still be managing if I hadn't met Donny Royce Patterson."

The name dried Syd's mouth as if she'd stuffed it full of cotton. She emptied the bottle of water and turned it over and over in her hands, her heart hammered as she dreaded where her story had to go from here.

"It was a couple years after Anthony died. The girls and I were getting along. We had lean times, and better times, but never affluent times. Sara had just turned fifteen, and Ginny was nine. Ginny had a softball tournament, and Sara and I were in the bleachers cheering for her team. This guy sat down in front of us. A younger guy, very good looking, and by himself. Ginny hit a homerun, and Sara and I were jumping up and down and screaming for her to run. When she crossed home plate, we hugged each other like crazy people. Sara stumbled and sent this guy's soda flying.

"It hit the ground, not him, thank goodness, and I offered to buy him another. He refused, but he kept up a conversation with the both of us through the rest of the game. Before we knew it, he'd introduced himself and moved up to sit with us. Once the game was over and Ginny joined us, he offered to buy a pizza. This was during one of those lean times, and pizza out was not in the budget. Both of the girls begged me to accept, and I didn't see the harm. He'd buy a pizza, we'd have a nice chat, he'd go about his business."

Mac leaned back on her elbows and rubbed the small protrusion of her belly. "I'm guessing it didn't go that way."

Syd shook her head. "I've wished a million times it had been that simple." She got to her feet, tossed the bottle in the trash, and circled the room. "Donny was a perfect gentlemen that night and all the nights that followed. He was ten years younger than I was.

That bothered me at first, but it didn't matter to him. He told me that the girls and I were the best thing that ever happened to him. He claimed age was just a number that hearts needed to ignore."

"Smooth," Randy said.

Syd snorted. The sound held no humor. "You don't know the half of it. Donny always knew just what to say. Maybe I was just old and lonely, but he made me feel things I'd thought were gone for good. Anthony was everything I'd ever wanted, and now there was this huge hole in all our lives. Donny seemed to fit right in. He was good to me and affectionate with the girls. He took their side in almost every argument—"

"You didn't find that strange?" Jesse finally broke her silence.

Syd swung around to face her. "In retrospect, yes. But at the time..." She raised her hands. "Anthony was the same way. A real pro when it came to getting what he and the girls wanted regardless of what I thought. Kittens, getting their ears pierced, a snack before dinner. It was always three against one. I actually thought it was sweet that Donny did the same." The words left a bitter taste in Syd's mouth, and she snagged a second bottle of water. "We married three months later. Donny lost his job a month after that."

"Con man," Charley whispered.

Syd looked at Charley. "And a drug user, a liar, and a free-loader, and a couple of other things I found out about too late."

"Scum," Randy said.

Syd gave her the point and continued, "He brought his own set of bills to the marriage, and his added to mine made a tight financial situation worse. For the first time in my life, I needed a job. I took the first one I could find, working in a local grocery store covering shifts no one else wanted. Donny became Mr. Mom."

A small gasp came from somewhere, but Syd ignored it.

"Things seemed to settle down for the next couple of months. We were keeping afloat financially, and Donny went out of his way to be helpful. The house payment needed to be made? No problem, he'd make it while he was out *looking for a job*. Electricity due? He'd swing by the utilities department—no need for me make an extra trip. It wasn't until later that I learned just how far behind he'd put us."

"He wasn't paying the bills?" Randy asked.

"Very few of them. I found out after the cops took him away that a lot of the money I gave him for bills was going to buy pills and pot. Pot he was sharing with Sara."

Charley narrowed her eyes, all cop. "You weren't suspicious?"

"Why would I be? On the surface, everything seemed fine. He was home when the mail came every day and made sure the stack was purged of anything he didn't want me to see." Syd stopped and rubbed her temples, gathering herself for the story to come. *Father, help me make them see.*

"So, I'm working, and Donny is *looking* and playing housekeeper in his spare time. Things began to shift at home, things I didn't understand until later. Sara became rebellious and Ginny grew distant. I tried to talk to both of them but didn't get anywhere. Ginny just kept to her room, and Sara gravitated more and more to Donny. I was worried, but so much had changed for them. Losing Anthony, Donny becoming a part of our lives, me working for the first time." Syd hugged her arms around herself, her voice barely a whisper. "I know in hindsight that it was more than that. I should have dug deeper, but blaming those things made sense. If someone had walked up to me and told me that Donny and Sara..." Her breath caught in her throat, and she couldn't say the words. "That there was something going on between my husband and my daughter, I would have laughed at them. Things like that didn't happen in the world I lived in." Her voice cracked. "I was stupid as well as blind."

Randy put her hand over her heart. "Oh, no."

Alex slipped an arm around her shoulders. "Sometimes we can't comprehend evil if we've never seen it."

"Exactly," Syd said.

Jesse leaned forward and spoke for the first time. "Hold on a second. Donny and Sara were..." Her eyes went wide. "And you think Mason... How could you?"

"I know he didn't..." Syd looked at her friend. "I don't expect you to forgive me, but please hear me out."

Jesse pressed her lips into a tight line and sat back without another word, but her indignant gaze never wavered from Syd's face.

Alex squeezed her shoulders. "Tell us the rest."

Syd gathered her courage, sat back down, and plowed into the final chapter of her story. "I came home from work one Friday afternoon, and Ginny was home alone. I asked her where everyone was, and she said that Sara had gone out with some school friends and Donny had gone to get burgers for dinner. Donny was home before long, and we ate and watched a couple of movies. Sara's Friday night curfew was ten. Ten came and went, and so did eleven with no word. By then I was furious with her. By midnight, furious became frantic." The memory of her panic sent Syd back to her feet.

"Ginny had gone to bed, and Donny was trying to calm me down. I suggested calling the police, and he said we needed to give her a little more time. By two a.m. I was a wreck, and he offered to go look for her. Always the caring husband and father." The words were bitter. "He convinced me to stay at the house. Someone needed to stay with Ginny, and what if Sara came home, and we were both gone?"

"You must have been out of your mind with worry," Mac said.

"It was the longest night of my life. When he hadn't returned by nine in the morning, I called the cops. They took some information and put out some alerts, but I could tell they weren't taking this as seriously as I wanted them to."

"We see runaway teens every day," Charley said.

"I almost wish she had run away." Syd's voice cracked on the words. "Sometime after lunch that day, a maid at some fleabag hotel in the next town recognized Sara from one of the alerts. She called the cops. When they got there, they found Donny and Sara together."

"Oh, Syd." Alex's eyes were full of sympathetic tears.

"They arrested Donny and took Sara to the hospital. A counselor managed to get most of story out of her, but the damage was done. On Monday of that week, the electricity was shut off. The same day, I got notified that my car was about to be repo'd. I couldn't believe it. I scoured the house and found a stack of old notices in the back of one of his drawers along with a bag of pot. It was like his final chance to say 'Look what an idiot you are.' We found out two weeks later that Sara was pregnant."

"Oh, Syd." Jesse's face finally held some sympathy.

"What about Ginny?" Mac asked.

"Anthony's parents had her by this time. She was a wreck, and I was a wreck. At first I was grateful for their help. But once the whole story came out, they hired a lawyer and sued for custody. They wanted both girls, but Sara refused. Told them she would run away if they forced the issue. She was old enough that the court took her preference into consideration."

"That's when you moved to Garfield," Randy said.

"That's when. With a very pregnant daughter and my tail between my legs, looking for a new beginning" She looked at Randy. "You gave me a place to start to heal, and when you guys made me a part of your circle, I knew you loved me, but I couldn't share the story. I was so embarrassed and ashamed. I'd lost Ginny. More important than any repercussions that might have come back on me, I wanted Sara to raise her son without the stigma of everything that happened hanging over her head."

"Did Sara ever say what did happen?" Charley asked.

"Probably not anything you haven't heard," Syd told her. "Donny used me to get to her. At first, he threatened her. Told her if she didn't do what he wanted he'd hurt me or Ginny.

Then once he had his way, he convinced her that I'd hate her if I knew the truth. Add in the pot, and it only gets more complicated. She wanted to tell me, but she was ashamed and afraid. He eventually convinced her that he loved her. They were getting ready to disappear when the cops picked him up." Syd shook her head, her mouth pressed into a thin line. "He held me while I cried, and all the time he was planning their getaway."

Syd's legs wouldn't hold her up any longer, and she came back to the mat. "I loved my daughter then, and I love her now, but do you guys have any idea what it's like to look at your child and imagine...? There were days I wanted to shake her and ask her how she could have done this thing. Mostly, I just wondered how I'd been so gullible."

"Unbelievable," Alex said.

Jesse crossed her arms. "Its horrible, but I still don't understand why you'd think Mason would...I mean..."

Syd closed her eyes, took in a breath, and filled in the final pieces of the story. From Sara's mis-interpretation of what she saw following Ginny's breakup, to Ginny's account of what had actually happened. She mopped her face with a tissue. "Mason was trying to help. Sara and I were out of line, and I'm sorry."

"Ginny coming home unexpectedly, Logan so ill, the stress of not knowing what was going to happen there, and Sara's accusation. A perfect storm." Randy said.

"And then some," Syd agreed. "And I was blaming myself for what was happening to Sara and Logan."

"Why would you?" Alex asked.

"I thought God was still punishing me."

"Syd, that's just wrong," Mac told her.

"I know that, on most days. Nevertheless..."

The women moved as one to surround Syd. The tears they shared as they huddled were as freeing as the truth. A heavy load lifted from Syd's shoulders as she embraced her friends one by one. When Jesse held out her arms, Syd closed her eyes and stepped into the hug.

"I thought you'd hate me," Syd whispered.

"Hush," Jesse told her. "We're sisters."

Finally, they stood in a tight circle, hands clasped. "Can you guys forgive me?" Syd asked.

"You're already forgiven." Alex told her, "But let's make it official." She closed her eyes. "Father, thank You for Syd. Calm her heart and remove the last dregs of hurt and guilt from her life. Be there for her when Satan tries to slap her back with a past that you've forgotten. Restore unity among her and her daughters. Give them back the family ties that Satan worked so hard to break. Give her courage in You. Remind her every day how much she is loved by You and by us. Father, give her the words she needs to make things right with Mason. Soften his heart. He's hurt, we understand, but You have a plan for all of us. Have Your way in this situation."

Syd opened her eyes, blinded by the tears she'd refused to shed during the telling of her story. "You guys are... I don't think I have words for what you guys mean to me. I love you all. I was so afraid you'd walk away."

"Not a chance," Jesse said.

Syd and Jesse shared a look. "I want you to know that Mason is my next stop. He's been so good to me. He deserves an apology. I would have gone there first, but it's early and I knew you guys would all be here." That stupid cloth hovered in her thoughts once again. Syd gulped, seeing things clearly for the first time. Not another betrayal. God had tried to give her Mason's strong shoulders to lean on during one of the toughest days of her life, and Syd had allowed her past to send her in the opposite direction.

* * *

Mason snapped the leash onto Brody's collar while the dog wiggled with eagerness, barked, and pulled him toward the door. "Settle down, boy." He opened the front door and stopped short. Syd was standing on his porch, finger poised to ring the bell. *Explained the dog's excitement.* Brody lunged for Syd, and she bent down to take his head in her hands.

"Hey, Brody. Mind if I borrow your owner for a few minutes?" Syd looked up, pleading in her eyes. "I came to apologize... if you'll hear me out."

Mason stared at her. What was he supposed to do, shut the door in her face? He pulled the dog back into the house and stood to the side while Syd entered. All the while the dog danced in eager circles around his feet. "Give me a second, will you? I'll let him out the back."

He led the dog into the kitchen, unlocked the back door, and let Brody out. Mason stood there for several seconds, lost in thought. Syd wanted to apologize. He hadn't expected that. Wasn't even sure he wanted it.

Listen to what she has to say.

He looked up. "I probably know most of it," he muttered. But he headed back into the living room.

Syd stood just inside the door, bag clutched in her hands like a shield.

He motioned to the sofa. "Have a seat."

"No, this won't take long." She took a deep breath. "Like I said. I wanted to apologize for the other day. Sara...well, Sara has some traumatic things in her past. We both do. My second husband..."

Mason held up a hand, not happy with her, but not heartless enough to make her to go through the whole story for his benefit. "I know about Donny Patterson. I know what he did to Sara."

Syd tilted her head in question. "Did Jesse call you?"

"I was...disturbed by what you said Wednesday night, so I

looked some things up on the internet when I got home. I found the articles."

She nodded. "That's fair, I guess." Her feet shuffled, and the grip on her bag tightened. "Mason, I don't have words. When Sara saw you and Ginny outside the hospital Wednesday afternoon, she misread the situation. We were both sick with worry, worry that was making us a little crazy. I don't know if that will make what happened any easier for you to forgive, but if it helps, I'll tell you she was trying to protect her sister. That her efforts went horribly wrong is my fault, not hers." She met his gaze. "I hope someday you can find it in your heart to forgive both of us. I'd like us to be friends, but I know that you're going to need some time to get past all this."

She hesitated as if waiting for him to speak. What, exactly, was he supposed to say?

Syd nodded and her lips trembled in a small smile. "I really miss our talks. Will you call me sometime?"

For all the frustration of the last day, the sorrow on Syd's face tugged at his heart. He itched to hold her and found it necessary to clasp his hands behind his back to keep from giving in to the urge. Instead, he studied her. He understood what had happened on Wednesday and why, but did it really change anything? Did he want it to change things? Could he trust her to trust him? After what she'd been through, was trust even an option for her?

Father, show me how to help her.

Syd straightened her shoulders and turned for the door. "Well, OK, then. I'll get out of your hair."

Be her friend.

"Syd."

Syd turned. But instead of the beautiful woman he'd considered making a life with, a scarred and bent apparition stood at the door. He gasped at the sight. What?

Son, this is the picture my daughter sees when she looks in the mirror. So many scars inflicted by people she trusted, bent by the weight of a guilt she can't carry. I need you to help Me make her whole.

Mason blinked and Syd, the real Syd, stood before him, hands clasped at her waist, uncertainty etched into her features.

There is more than friendship here, son.

Mason heard the words in his heart. Felt them sink in and take hold. God, or wishful thinking? Did it matter? He moved forward and took Syd's hands in his. "I can be your friend."

Tears filled Syd's eyes, and she looked down.

He nudged her chin up until their eyes met once again. "But I'd like the option to explore something more in the future." He wrapped her in his arms and placed a gentle kiss on her lips. "I want the opportunity to erase Donny's treachery from your heart. I want the opportunity to show you that some men...that I...can be worthy of your trust. Will you give me that option, Sydney? I know you've been hurt by love. Will you let me show you that love can heal?"

"That's a pretty big challenge."

"I think I can handle it." He lowered his head and took her mouth with his. When he gave in to the kiss, he saw Syd's scars healing right before his eyes.

EPILOGUE

*S*ix months later

SYD SAT in the front row of the auditorium at Grace Community. She watched Mac replace the microphone and waddle from the stage. As nervous as Syd was, the sight made her smile. There were twins behind that waddle, one of each. Mac didn't get out much these days, but she'd vowed not to miss Alex's conference even if she had to be rolled onto the platform in a hospital bed.

Alex came to the podium. "Thanks for that lovely testimony, Mac. I know what a challenge it was for you to be here."

Syd squeezed Sara's hand, which was clasped in hers. Alex's conference had turned into a two-day affair.

Callie Stillman had shared a lovely story of listening to God even when you were sure He was wrong. Pam Lake gave them a beautiful story of forgiveness. Scottlyn Weber told about her rape and the baby she bore against her family's wishes—and the lovely family she'd been given as a result.

There were more people on the program. Charley was going

to talk about the importance of honesty in adoption, Jesse would share about spousal abuse, and Randy would give her testimony about her abusive childhood, but those were for after lunch. Now it was Syd's turn. Syd's and Sara's.

Alex cleared her throat. "You guys ready?"

They nodded in unison and got to their feet. A tug on her left hand held Syd in place. She looked down at Mason, the only male face in a room packed with women. He'd refused to let her come alone. In the last six months, he'd fulfilled his promises. He'd healed the parts of her heart she'd considered forever broken. Logan was already calling him Gramps. And the girls? They loved him, and he loved them. Mason had shown them a godly love, and everyone in her family needed more of that.

"I love you." He kissed the ring he'd put on her finger the week before. "Knock 'em dead."

I love you, too, she mouthed. Then she climbed the steps to the platform.

Alex beamed. "Ladies, you are in for a double treat. Let me introduce Sydney Patterson and her daughter, Sara Marlin. They have a touching story and a testimony that I know will minister to you." She handed the mic to Sydney.

She could do this. She would tell this assembly about how God had given her and Sara the strength to overcome impossible odds. Nobody should live with guilt and betrayal weighing down their hearts.

"Ladies, in Isaiah sixty-one, the Bible talks about giving us beauty for ashes, the oil of joy for mourning, the garment of praise for the spirit of heaviness. That's the story we want to share with you today."

Made in United States
Orlando, FL
14 July 2023

35127184R00114